ICELAND

ALSO BY RON BRIGGS

Yellow Hair Series

Erik Haraldsson

Tor's Saga

Cass

Westward

Journey to Iceland

ICELAND

YELLOW HAIR
BOOK SIX

RON BRIGGS

WOLFPACK
PUBLISHING
— EST 2013 —

Iceland
Paperback Edition
Copyright © 2025 by Ron Briggs

Wolfpack Publishing
1707 E. Diana Street
Tampa, Florida 33609

www.wolfpackpublishing.com

All rights reserved. No part of this book may be reproduced in any form or by any electronic or mechanical means, including information storage and retrieval systems, without express written permission from the publisher, except for the use of brief quotations in reviews. Any use of this publication to train generative artificial intelligence (AI) technologies is expressly prohibited.

This book is a work of fiction. References to historical events, real people, or real places are used fictitiously. Any similarity to real persons, living or dead, is purely coincidental and not intended by the author.

All brand names and product names used in this book are trademarks, registered trademarks, or trade names of their respective holders. Wolfpack Publishing is not associated with any product or vendor in this book.

Paperback ISBN 979-8-89567-141-2
Ebook ISBN 979-8-89567-140-5
LCCN 2024952437

FOREWORD

This is a work of fiction. The characters, events, and places are conceived by the author. Any references and actions by historical persons or places is fictionalized. An honest attempt has been made to describe real cultures and interactions as they may have taken place early in the eleventh century CE.

The story sets an example of how an Indigenous North American woman could have made her way to Iceland to provide the mitochondrial DNA markers found in a small population of Icelanders today.

This segment of the story illustrates some of the realities that woman, and her family, might have faced after they arrived in Iceland in 1030 CE. We follow Tor and Heidi as they learn to navigate the hate of some of their neighbors while their family grows, and the farm prospers. As the children mature, they are compelled to learn to deal with the same issues their parents were forced to endure. Tor's steady guidance and Heidi's strength of character guide the family through several trials, both physical and legal.

The descriptions of actions at the Althing are based on translations from various sagas written about two hundred years after this story takes place. The author hopes the reader finds the interpretation accurate and entertaining.

ICELAND

CHAPTER 1
ALTHING WORRIES

"The first step in the process is to meet with Garmr Hallrsson. He is the gothi for this district. To be successful we will need to win his support, along with his two freemen that sit on the district gothar at the Thorsnesthing and also on the full Gothar at the Althing over midsummer at Thingvalr. We will need to win this case in the *logretta*, or judicial, part of the Althing. An exception to a countrywide law is not an easy undertaking," Thorkell explained to Tor while they worked on combing sheep in the early spring.

"I never knew love could be so complicated." Tor sighed.

"You and Heidi have taught me that your wife

is a fine person in anybody's world. She is intelligent, hardworking, spiritual, and is ready to be a warrior when she or her loved ones are threatened —just as a Norse woman should be. Now, we must convince the gothar of that. Not easy, but I pray, not impossible."

"Sounds like we need to get started as soon as possible."

"Yes, you and I will take the wagon to Garmr's farm tomorrow morning. I cannot say when the law in question was enacted, but I suspect it was before you left Ulfrstadt. I am sure Garmr will have the details," Thorkell finished the conversation.

The next morning, Tor was in the barn feeding extra grain to the two horses they would harness to the wagon for the three-hour trip to Hallrlandstedr. Tor was nervous and anxious to get Heidi approved for citizenship in Iceland.

"Come, husband, you need your feed as much as the horses do. Hildr and I have a hearty meal of roast lamb, boiled turnips, and wheat gruel waiting for you. Thorkell has just sat down, so you better hurry," Heidi admonished Tor. She could see the worry in his eyes and put her arm around him as she dragged him from the horse stall. *Please ease his worried mind, Great One Above. I know you have the power. He never stopped worshipping You while he was on Turtle Island where no one knows you. But Tor has always called you his God—show him you are listening, please. Amen.*

They walked hand in hand to the kitchen in the great hall. As soon as Heidi was in sight, baby Gerna started crying for her mama. Heidi's warm breast soothed the child instantly.

———

"JUST TELL the gothi your story as you have told Hildr and me. You need not embellish anything. The truth is simple—keep it that way," Thorkell told Tor when Garmr's hall came into view.

The farm was an idyllic setting with the stone and sod hall standing a short distance from a low stone barn. From the hall, it was a short walk down to a small lake. A few shade trees still stood to the far end of the lake. Waterfowl swam in family groups around the lake while sheep grazed on the opposite hillside.

"I am so nervous, I may not be able to talk at all," Tor blurted out.

"Just relax. Confidence will be your ally."

A thrall came to the intricately carved wooden

door on the east side of the hall. "Greetings, Thorkell Rolfcarlsson, please come in and wait in the entry while I fetch the Master. Can I tell him the nature of your visit?" said the thrall, with a Gaelic accent.

"Thank you, Albert. We are here on business for the Thorsnesthing," Thorkell replied.

"Yes, of course. Please wait here, and I with bring Garmr Hallrsson, *gothi* of Thornes district."

Soon the servant and master returned and ushered Thorkell and Tor to the main table. Garmr sat in a high chair that was intricately carved with pagan and Christian symbols.

"Welcome to Hallrlandstedr, Thorkell Rolf-carlsson. I see you have brought your nephew, the storied Tor Eriksson. Am I to assume your business concerns this young man?" Garmr asked.

"Yes, allow me to introduce you. Garmr Hallrs-son, Gothi of Thornes District, I present Tor Eriks-son, son of my deceased nephew, Erik Haraldsson. Tor is the last of my living kinfolk," Thorkell said reverently.

"Pleased to meet you, Gothi Garmr," Tor said, managing to sound confident.

"You are quite the traveler, if the stories I have

been told hold any credence," Garmr replied in a cordial manner.

"I am in the dark about what stories you may have heard, but yes, I have traveled a great distance, though much of it not of my choosing."

"And what service do you seek of my position this day?"

Tor was taken aback at the speed the gothi got to the reason they were in his presence. "If you know my story, you know that many of us from Ulfrstadt were on a voyage to Greenland to find farms and settle in the young colony. Father had planned to stay for three days in Iceland to allow the settlers who had never been on the sea a respite on land before the final sail to Greenland. The coast of Iceland was in sight when that first storm hit and drove us far off course..."

"Yes, I recall that storm. It was vicious here on land as well. That was several years past. You must have been quite young," Garmr interrupted.

After three hours of telling his story and answering questions for Gothi Garmr, Tor was exhausted.

"As I see it, there is no reason for my services, Tor Eriksson. Despite the rumors that abound, at this time there is no specific law preventing you from marrying a woman from Vinland. True, it is highly frowned upon, and the Church does not recognize Skræling as real people, therefore they would not sanctify your marriage. However, you have said your wife has been baptized, along with your children. I can see no further legal action that needs to be taken," Garmr stated.

"This is a great relief to me, Gothi Garmr," Tor replied.

"Be aware, young man, just because you have broken no countrywide laws here in Iceland, you will not be free from the consequences of bringing a Skræling to this land. There is much ill will toward Skræling across the island. Rumors were started, when Vinland was discovered, that a law regarding Skræling marriage had been established. However, that is not true. Some use that rumor to intimidate people from forming mixed marriages with the very few thralls that have been brought here and producing mixed-race children. And, as you know, Norsemen have been wounded and some killed in Vinland. There are those that will think a blood debt still needs to be paid."

"As I understand it, more of the Vinlanders have been killed than Norsemen. Should that not settle all blood debts?" Tor asked.

"Not necessarily. Remember, more than your family's ships have disappeared in the waters west of here over the years. Many argue the heathens you so adamantly defend are responsible for at least some of those disappearances. Most who live here have never and will never see a Skræling. But word is out that you brought one to this country. Some will see your family as vermin that need to be exterminated.

"I am not telling you this to make you fear for your lives every day. But you need to be aware that those feelings are out there, and caution would be prudent. Your wife is the only one of her race I have heard of living in this district. Gradually, you should fit in and all will be fine. But there may be some ugly times, as well. Do you understand?" Garmr's tone was serious, and he kept hard eye contact with Tor.

"It is as Wolf told Heidr Tungl," Tor said, as much to himself as to answer Garmr.

"Excuse me, what did you say? Who is Wolf?" Garmr asked.

"Long story. My wife's people believe that each person is given an animal spirit helper, who, more or less, guides them through hard times. Sort of like the old pagan myths of the Norse. Wolf, or

First Man, is Heidi's spirit helper. She says he told her she would face hate and danger in the lands of my people, and he would not be able to cross the sea to stand with her," Tor answered, wishing he had not mentioned Wolf in the first place.

"Well, whatever all that means, just keep a watchful eye out."

"I will Gothi Garmr," Tor replied.

"I believe we have used up the day. You will not get home before dark. I can have my housemaid send some food with you," Garmr told Tor.

Tor looked over at Thorkell who was sound asleep in a chair. "We brought a basket with food, so we will be all right. Sorry for taking up your day for my foolish worries," Tor responded as he stood and stepped toward his uncle.

"Not a problem for me. Answering legal questions is what I do. I will have my stable servant bring your wagon from the barn so you can get on the road while you deal with Thorkell."

"Thank you for your hospitality, Gothi Garmr."

Garmr excused himself and left the room. Tor roused Thorkell and after another round of thank you and farewells, they were soon headed back to Thorkell's farm.

CHAPTER 2

MEMORIES

Three evenings after Tor and Thorkell met with the gothi, Tor and Heidi had the children settled down to sleep. As a habit, when they got into their own bed, they talked quietly in the Monongahela tongue. They did so to discuss their private affairs, knowing no one else understood their conversations. Young Erik could understand most of it, but he was fast asleep in another room.

Often, these conversations led to muffled love-making episodes. This night, Tor put his arm around Heidi and held her tight to his side. She immediately sensed he had something serious to discuss.

"What is it, husband? Are you well?"

Looking straight up into the darkness, Tor replied, "Yellow Hair believes Bright Moon must consider Yellow Hair a fool for dragging her from the ancestral lands to this place, where many consider her less than a human being. Now, it seems we are trapped here and may never find peace. Yellow Hair carries a great guilt for doing this to his precious Bright Moon."

"At this moment, Bright Moon is more concerned that Yellow Hair has a short memory. She can recall standing on a riverbank, eyes locked with Yellow Hair's and witnessing the twining of souls as they danced in the ethereal light in Yellow Hair's bottomless pools of liquid blue sky. In that first meeting, those life-souls became one, and made vows to one another that they would never separate. No hill, no mountain, no valley, no river, no ocean, no spirit, no lords of Cahokia, nor no God would ever force them to part. This is what Bright Moon remembers. What memory does Yellow Hair carry?" She turned on her side, pushed closer into his side, and looked to his face in the darkness for reaction.

"As always, Bright Moon is right. She has always shown more wisdom than her bumbling husband!" He turned into her and pressed his lips against hers. In seconds their linen night clothes were off, and they were locked in love's embrace until each was satisfied, out of breath, and covered with sweat.

"Now, we will waste no more time talking of 'could have been' and work to make the future better for our family?" Heidi asked softly in Norse.

"Yes, my love," Tor replied, pulling their sweaty bodies closer. Their lips met again, and soon the earlier activity was repeated.

Breathing heavily, Heidi said, "I remember our first coupling. It was my first experience, and you had only known one other, so we were both clumsy and did not perform like we just did. But that experience brought us closer together. Since then, we have become masters. But I will never share my skills with anyone but you. I promise you that. I will die before another man touches me."

"I would die before another man touches you. I promise you that—even if it was your choice. And, for me, no other woman exists," Tor replied. Her kiss told him he better get ready for another round of lovemaking.

The next day was a quiet one on the farm. Heidi had finally got Gerna down for an afternoon nap, and Erik was in the barn helping a new mama tend to a newborn lamb. Hildr implored Heidi and Tor to tell some of their stories from Vinland.

They began by telling about canoeing down the Spirit River and learning to play chunkey at Squirrel Tail Village. By the time they got far into the story, Thorkell was sound asleep in his high chair. Hildr was spellbound listening and paid no attention to her husband. Heidi looked to the old man with his slackened face and line of drool down his chin with worry in her souls.

Hildr made it a daily routine that after midday meal, there would be some time set aside for story-telling. She especially seemed to enjoy the days when Thorkell and Tor were busy with something outside the hall—her time spent with Heidi telling of crossing the mountains in late pregnancy and then giving birth to Erik in Sun Town. Hildr claimed it was her way of coping after all she had lost. Now and then, she would flash worried eyes to her sleeping husband whenever he was present, but never said a word about it.

Heidi recited many of the stories she and Tor had shared in villages after they left Cahokia. She refrained from telling the battle with the war chief, Ganeco on the Juniata River. Likewise, she avoided all her stories that involved killing. Heidi felt and understood Hildr's desire to hear stories with happy endings. She had enough of those to keep the older woman listening, even repeating lighter stories on occasion to keep Hildr smiling.

When Thorkell and Tor were in attendance, Heidi turned the speaking over to Tor. He generally talked about Heidi's hunting prowess and described her harvesting some large animal using stealth, outwitting the animal, then making an incredible bowshot to quickly dispatch her prey. How, after each kill, she would talk to the downed animal, asking forgiveness and praying to her creator to hurry the creature's soul to the afterlife. Hildr seemed to especially enjoy that spiritual aspect of Heidi's hunting skills.

CHAPTER 3

EGILL AND CAIRENN

When Bjarni's ship landed in Brattahlid, the days were longer than the nights, and the weather was fair with progressively warming days and cold nights. Still, cold rain or even snow were possible at any time. Surprise storms were always a hazard in the North Atlantic.

Hryn waited for Egill to come up the path from the dock, but Cairenn was nowhere in sight. His heart sank. But he had to know if Cairenn had married another, so he approached Hryn.

"About time you showed up, you worthless piece of human flotsam!" Hryn called out when he was still several paces away.

"What have I done, Hryn Reginnswife?" His heart pounding in his chest.

"You know as well as you are breathing what you did. And no word from you all winter? Do you think she wants to have that child with no father? What is wrong with you?" Her tongue was wound up and would not stop throwing insults at him. "How many other bastard children and husband-less mothers have you left behind?"

"Hryn, Hryn, I know not what you are saying. Is Cairenn with child? Could it be mine? Oh, blessed are the saints! I was coming to ask her hand in marriage. But I know nothing of a child," Egill stammered.

"That is right, you know nothing. God gave you that worm to make babies, not satisfy your own lust. What did you think would happen when you planted your worthless seed in that poor, innocent girl? You should be castrated and hung in the square!

"But then if you are willing to make an honest, Christian wife of her...I suppose...but what of your life? You are always at sea. No life for a young mother."

She thought of her own life. Married to a man

of the sea. Only home long enough to get her pregnant, then help bury the child a year or two later. Their three children had been born sickly. Only one lived more than a year, but little more. She did not want that for Cairenn. Cairenn was a wedding gift from her parents. Cairenn's mother had been their house servant in Norway before they moved to Iceland, and then to Greenland. Cairenn was born in Greenland when Hryn was not yet a married woman. She felt complete responsibility for the humble, hardworking girl.

"No, you may not marry her as long as you belong to the sea. The sea is your mistress. I do know a shipwright in Gardar, however. I think he could use a hand. If you are worth your eagerness to bed my servant, you will seek local work and forgo your lust for the sea."

"Do you mean it, Hryn? I will gladly forsake the sea for Cairenn. She is the one love of my life. But Bjarni has me under his power. How will I get out of that? Perhaps after this voyage to Vinland?" Egill questioned.

"This village and Gardar are crawling with young single men who want to go to sea, and some seasoned ones as well. I am sure Bjarni will have no issue replacing you. Now, go find employment and square with Bjarni before you come back to visit my house. And mind you, Reginn Engarsson has not yet sailed, you will be proper around Cairenn," Hryn admonished Egill.

"Thank you, thank you, thank you!" he shouted. He put his hand on her shoulder and started back toward the dock.

"Wait, what news of Heidi and Tor have you brought? A man representing Leif Eriksson came here right after you sailed for Iceland last fall. He had questions for them. Did they return on Bjarni's ship? What about her babe?" Hryn fired questions faster than Egill could answer them.

"They are alive and healthy. The baby girl arrived at midwinter and is named Gerna after Tor's deceased sister. She has brown hair and those haunting black eyes like Heidi. But her skin is pink and soft. She is a beautiful babe. Tor's uncle, Thorkell Rolfcarlsson is insisting that Tor is the rightful heir to Rolfcarllandstedr and will take over operations as Thorkell slows down. Their future looks bright."

Within a month, Egill and Cairenn were married and living in a tiny house close to Hryn's hall. Every day Egill took a ferry cross Eriksfjord and walked the short distance to the shipworks in Gardar. Cairenn continued her work as Hryn's housemaid. Her duties lessened as her pregnancy advanced to its final stages.

———

THE SCOUTS WATCHED the great canoe come to a stop a safe distance from shore. The moon was but a sliver, and the stars were mostly obscured by high, thin clouds. The vessel was hard, but not impossible to see. Bull Moose had ordered all fires extinguished, so no lights appeared in the bay or on the surrounding land.

It was late at night, and Bjarni did not want to disturb Bull Moose at that hour. The longhouses were still, dark mounds, barely discernible in the forest, and no voices were heard. The village appeared abandoned. *I should have landed closer to the mouth of the bay and come in in the morning. Well, we are here now. Perhaps, they are all asleep—no need for guards around this outpost!*

The ship settled into quiet stillness after a heavy rope lowered the anchor stone to the bottom of the bay. Tomorrow Bjarni would bargain with Bull Moose for more trees. He took Tor's advice and brought more valuable trade goods that were sure to win the favor of Bull Moose and the Micmac people.

After the Norsemen had settled into complete silence, four bark canoes approached in complete silence. A thickening overcast sky helped hide the dark canoes sliding slowly across the dark water. When they pulled alongside, reed brushes were used to saturate the wood planks just above the waterline with boiled pine pitch. The heavy, cold air kept the scent of the pine oil near the water's surface. As soon as both sides of the ship were wetted, a warrior on each side opened a small carved stone container with hot coals in it. A torch dipped in pine tar was touched to the hot coals, then the flaming torch quickly slid down the length of the ship, igniting the smeared pine oil. The hull of the ship was engulfed in flames while the canoes rapidly fled.

Bull Moose stood on the shore and watched the ship burn and listened to the screaming sailors as they jumped into the frigid waters of the bay. Only two Norsemen were able to make it to the shore alive, and they were shot many times with arrows, never getting out of the water. "Humph! I warned him not to return." Bull Moose scowled. Parts of the ship still smoldered at dawn as water seeped into the burned-out hull at the waterline. No word ever reached Greenland or Iceland as to the fate of Bjarni's final voyage to Vinland.

CHAPTER 4
INHERITANCE

One day in late May, Tor was working on a worn bridle when Thorkell tottered over to him, looked at his work, and said, "Fine job, Gunnar, you are becoming a man."

Stunned, Tor looked up and said, "Uncle, I am Tor."

Thorkell replied, "Yes, yes, of course." He had an odd, questioning look in his eye and a crooked smile. He just walked away to the hall.

"Are you feeling all right, uncle?" Tor called out to him. Thorkell did not look back, just turned his head slightly and raised his hand dismissively.

That night Tor talked it over with Hildr when

Thorkell had fallen asleep in his chair. "You are just noticing?" she asked. "His mind has been slipping of late. His memory is failing. I fear his long life is coming to an end. It has been a good life, a bittersweet life. He has known great prosperity, and tragic loss. He misses our sons more than words can tell. And I know being the last of the Rolfcarlsson brothers has torn him from within. Family has always meant so much to him." A tear trickled down her cheek.

As spring faded into summer and farm work intensified with the cutting and storing of hay, harvesting the self-sown rice ripening near the water, harvesting the sown barley, tending livestock, Thorkell drew further and further into himself. Most times when he talked to people, he smiled, but was given to hateful bursts of bad temperament, especially in the late afternoon hours and particularly toward Erik and Hildr. With more and more frequency, he had difficulty remembering the smallest things. Oft times, he referred to Tor as Gunnar, his late son's name. He also began to wander aimlessly. His eyes lost their keen focus. Tor increasingly had to keep an eye on him when they were outside. On a couple of occasions, he was nearly to town before Tor caught up to him. "Just going to pick up the keel for a boat I am building," he told Tor on one such occasion.

Hildr cried herself to sleep late each night knowing her lifelong companion was slipping away from her. Lack of sleep and worry were taking their toll on her strong mind and body. Heidi spent her days trying to console and comfort the older woman. She had witnessed a few elders in her life who acted like Thorkell was. She recalled one instance where the man had no living relatives. He was given a bow and quiver, along with a flint knife, and allowed to wander off. No one ever saw him again. Sadness filled the hall that summer.

———

THORKELL DID MANAGE to go to the Althing at Thingvalr at midsummer. Many came to Thorkell with friendly greetings only to be politely dismissed because Thorkell did not recognize them. After three days of the fourteen-day festival, Thorkell said he was ready to go home.

"All these strangers...I wonder where my

friends have gone." Thorkell mused aloud when they left the grounds.

———

THE REST OF THE SUMMER, everyone kept a tight watch on Thorkell as he slipped farther from reality. Other than some herbal medicines that seemed to have no effect, no one knew how to treat the mind slipping sickness.

Early in the fall, Thorkell slipped away from the watchful eyes of the family. Tor was butchering a cow, Erik was helping all his four-summers old body would allow, Heidi was tending to Gerna's needs, and Hildr was at her loom, lost in depression.

While Thorkell wandered across the hills, a cold rain blew in from the north. When they discovered that Thorkell was missing, Tor saddled a horse and went down the lane to find him. He got all the way to Borg and found no one who had seen him. Ice was beginning to form on the vegetation. Back at the hall, no one had found Thorkell yet.

Shivering in a small copse of birch trees, Thorkell tried to fathom where he was and how he got there. *Where is Mother? She would never leave me here with these strange people. They will not even talk to me. This is a fine mess. I will just wait for Mother. She'll be here soon.* "Harald? Where are you? Sigurd, is that you? I'm over here. Why can't you see me? Haakon will be here soon, he'll be mad!" Darkness started to descend on him. *Wish I had a sheep, they are always warm.* His addled brain could not make sense of anything.

All the farm help, a few people from Borg, and Tor were combing the countryside as darkness fell. The freezing rain continued into the night, making the search increasingly difficult. Their world turned into a silvery, dreamlike landscape. Every step was a crunch. The only sound was the falling rain that froze on contact, building a thicker and thicker coating on everything exposed. The searchers carried oil torches that sputtered and smoked but gave off a pitifully small amount of light. The search went on late into the night, and the searchers came up empty. At some point, they gave up and went to the hall to warm up and rest until daybreak.

By dawn, the rain had stopped but the temperature remained below freezing. Without sleep, Tor saddled the horse again and set out across the fields. He tried to think of Thorkell's favorite places on the farm. He remembered a little spring in a gully in the middle of a large pasture. The spring was surrounded by a little copse of birch trees, and Thorkell said it produced the sweetest water in all of Iceland. It was more than three leagues from the hall, and Tor could not fathom how Thorkell would have gotten that far. He hoped against hope that someone in town had taken him in for the night.

Tor crested a hill and looked down on the little grove of trees. Somehow, he knew he would find Thorkell's body there. *What a lonely place for a great man to die,* he thought as he looked at the small trees bent from the heavy ice that clung to their branches. Tears streamed from Tor's eyes as he dismounted onto the crunchy grass next to the little trees. Thorkell's lifeless body sat propped against a small tree. Oddly, his face bore a crooked smile. *What was his last thought?* Tor cried as he lifted the stiff body. Tor was amazed at how light Thorkell had become. Nearly two years past when Tor arrived in Borg, Thorkell had been almost his size. Now he did not weigh half as much as he had then.

All of Borg turned out for Thorkell's funeral,

and many tributes to him were spoken to Hildr and Tor at the feast in Rolfcarllandstedr Hall. Tor was amazed at the outpouring of tribute for a man who had only lived among them for six or seven years. *He truly was a great man. Loved by all who knew him,* he proudly mused.

———

WINTER SET in with no word from Bjarni. Tor concluded that they had to go far to find a peaceful people to trade with. They must have had to overwinter in Vinland. He was convinced that the white, upturned hands painted on the bow of the ship and variety of trade goods that he had talked Bjarni into taking would win Bjarni favor with some people of Vinland, perhaps even someone who had known of Yellow Hair and Bright Moon. He still held on to his dream of peaceful trade routes being established, maybe even a trip with him and his family someday among the peoples he had met.

Late in the winter, Hildr died in her sleep. She had a smile on her face when Heidi found her in bed. Another funeral followed by an outpouring of love and honor for the deceased filled the hall.

After the hall emptied of the mourners, Tor and Heidi looked in on Erik and Gerna to find them sleeping peacefully. Heidi turned to Tor and said, "Sometimes when God takes a life, He gives a new one in its place." She held her hand on her belly and smiled. Tor hugged her. She felt a warm wetness on her cheek.

CHAPTER 5
TWINS

As the summer solstice approached, a ship arrived from Brattahlid. Tor, Heidi, and the children went to town to hear the news from Brattahlid. Perhaps there would be word of Bjarni. The first thing Heidi noticed was a woman with long, wavy, orange hair carrying a little girl with glowing red hair on her hip. Next to her was a plain dressed big man carrying a large bag. "Any rooms for guests from Brattahlid on these shores?" The man smiled at Heidi as he spoke.

"As long as I get to hold that beautiful child in my arms!" a very pregnant Heidi gushed.

"Granted!" Cairenn beamed, walked up, and plopped her child in Heidi's outstretched arms.

The little girl did not even fuss. Tor and Egill hugged and exchanged pleasantries.

"What is your name?" Heidi asked. The little girl dove her head into Heidi's neck, too shy to speak.

"Heidi Torswife, it would be my pleasure to introduce you to Heidi Hryn Egillsdottir," Cairenn announced. "I insisted we name her after the person who made her possible. And her middle name is for the woman who looks after us."

While they walked back to the hall, Heidi and Cairenn talked ceaselessly about what had transpired since they last saw each other.

Egill told Tor about his work repairing ships instead of rowing them. No word had come back yet regarding Bjarni's voyage to Vinland. People were speculating that Skræling ate Bjarni and all his men. Tor prayed that this summer would bring news.

Egill and Cairenn had gotten passage on the knorr owned by Thorstan Hrolfger of Brattahlid. "Thorimm Thorstansson told me to tell you that the Skræling woman would not be welcomed back in Brattahlid. His family owns the ship we came on. In fact, he, or rather his father, owns the shipworks where I work. He wanted me to deliver this message," Egill said nervously.

"It matters not, we go where we like. We have power too and do not quiver in front of some sniveling son of a supposed lord. We cannot allow unjust laws to stand, nor can we allow unjust men enforce those unjust laws," Tor said nonchalantly. "I think we have a lamb ready for the pot, do we not, Heidi?"

A few days after Egill and Cairenn arrived in Iceland, Heidi went into labor. Cairenn volunteered to serve as midwife and took charge. Heidi had informed her that she knew she was carrying two little ones and was anticipating a long and difficult delivery. She called on another woman from Borg to help Cairenn with the birth when the time came.

Heidi went through her normal energy spurt early that morning, but when she squatted to milk one of the two cows, her water broke. She lost her balance and plopped onto her back beside the gentle brown cow.

Cairenn was just getting started with milking the goats. Cairenn raised the alarm and soon Heidi was in her birthing bed with Cairenn attending to her while Egill and Tor were rushing to town to fetch Ingris Lauderfulmerswife to help deliver the babies. Before the sun went low in the western sky, Heidi held a new daughter at each breast.

One was born with a thick shock of black hair, light-colored eyes, and pink skin. The second child had only a few wisps of light-colored hair, almost black eyes, and darker colored skin. Tor insisted they be named Bjarta Stjarna, Bright Star, and Heidr Tungl, Bright Moon. Heidi was reluctant to give a daughter her own name, but finally acquiesced. Taking it further, Heidi argued that all her children should have Norse names to lessen their chance of being harassed due to their heritage.

Now it was Tor's turn to acquiesce. *Bjarta Stjarna* was given Tor's mother's namesake, Erna while Heidr Tungl was given Tor's grandmother's name, Gerdis. They would use the Monongahela names only within the family. Tor was uncomfortable making these concessions, but Heidi convinced him that they knew before they left Turtle Island that life would be hard for her. She willingly accepted those hardships to be at his side and would have it no other way. Giving her children Norse names was a small price for the children's future safety and happiness.

———

Heidi and Cairenn conspired to convince Egill to stay in Iceland and work on the farm. Tor sent a bag of silver coins to Hryn, in Greenland, on the ship that Egill and Cairenn were to sail on. The gesture was intended to allow Hryn to hire a new housemaid.

Tor and Egill worked well together, and the farm prospered, soon becoming one of the largest sheep farms in western Iceland. Tor's reputation as a fair and honest businessman producing fine wool and valuable sheep spread far and wide in western Iceland. Unknown to Tor, that was causing him a problem.

Ferrminn Homallarsson had inherited the former largest sheep ranch in western Greenland. Ferrminn had developed a strong like for ale and spent much of his time in the ale house in Borg bragging about his great farm and famous wool to all the sailors who came into the establishment when they were in port. The problem was, he was not doing his part to maintain the great farm his ancestors had built. The farm was in decline, and Ferrminn concluded that was mostly Tor Eriksson's fault. *Tor has a Skræling whore for a wife and should not be allowed to be a landholder at all.*

CHAPTER 6
ESUS

Six years had passed with no word regarding the fate of Bjarni Einarsson. Icelanders grew more and more convinced that Skræling were the cause. And although Tor's sheep, wool, and horse business was booming, they found the community distancing them socially. They were so busy with the farm, they had little time for socializing, so they barely noticed.

Tor invested some of his silver in a knorr to try to establish a trade relationship with his old friends. His pleas to gather a crew for a trading voyage to Turtle Island fell on an increasingly somber crowd. No one was interested in sailing to certain death. At no time was Tor able to gather more than fifteen men willing partake in the enterprise. Tor slowly relinquished his dream of a prosperous trade with his friends on the Lenape River. He put his energy into making the farm a more prosperous enterprise.

———

"Take your sisters to the back of the hall. Do not argue and keep them quiet." Heidi said quietly to eight-year-old Erik as she studied the figure coming up the lane on a big black horse. The man had long, flowing red hair and wore an expensive leather tunic of a design that said the man came from Ireland.

Erik grudgingly herded six-year-old Gerna, four-year-old Erna and Gerdis, and two-year-old Unndis into the playroom in the rear of the hall.

Heidi stood to the side of the hall entrance holding the hoe she had been using to chop weeds in her garden.

As the man approached, he stopped and folded his right leg over the saddle and spoke in broken Norse/Irish that was difficult to understand. "Oh, but aren't ye are a pretty one, lass? Just as the boys down at the dock told me. T'will be a pleasure having you."

"I am a Christian woman, married to the lord of this hall," she said confidently.

"No, lass, you are naught but a Skræling whore, and I plan to make good use of you," he boasted.

"Who are you? What are you doing here?" she demanded.

"It matters not to you who I am. You'll spread your brown legs and give me a go. I know how 'tis in these parts, and Skræling are offered no protection in any form. If you should raise even a word in protest, I can demand retribution from this estate. In fact, I believe I will take the whole damn thing." He jumped down from the horse and strode toward her.

"You are Esus from Dublin. My husband went to Borg with a wagonload of sheep to sell to you," she said as confidently as she could. She noted he carried a short riding whip in his hand. *He no doubt thinks he is going to use that on me. I wish I had my old warclub right now, instead of this puny hoe.*

"No sense in resisting, woman. Let's go get the deed over, and nobody gets hurt. Your husband will be working with my second for some time finalizing that sheep deal. I always wanted one of you brownies. Show me to your bed." He handled the whip in a menacing manner. She backed away from him.

He lunged at her, trying to snare the hoe with the whip. She dodged his advance and kicked him hard in the back quarter of his knee. He went down in pain, clutching his damaged leg.

"You fool!" he screamed. "Now I WILL own this farm!"

She stepped on his arm that held the whip and said, "No, you won't. You will get back on your horse and pretend you never came up that lane."

With speed she had never encountered, he rolled into her, knocking her off her feet. As she tried to scramble away from him, she felt the whip slash across her shoulder, ripping her dress and opening her skin. She wheeled and drove her foot into his stomach. When he doubled over, she jerked her knee up into his face. He shook it off and thrust a shoulder into her, tackling her. She thrashed, but he fought and gained control of her arms.

"I like a fighter! I've heard all you dark savages know is fighting," he exclaimed as he gripped her arms tightly above her shoulders. A leg forced itself between her thighs. She twisted under him, but he pressed his body against hers, making it difficult to move. She tried to wrap her leg around his sore knee. She was beginning to tire already. *I am in no condition to fight. I have been too lazy of late.*

Suddenly, his body went limp, and his grip loosened. She rolled him off of her to see Erik standing there with fireplace log in his hands.

"He was trying to hurt you, Mother." He held the club in a way that he could hit the man in the head if he moved.

"Thank you, son. Go get some twine so we can tie him up," she told Erik while she brandished the club over Esus.

When Esus awoke, he was bound against one of the tall posts next to the hall entrance. His head felt as if it had been cleaved in two. "Ye've done it now, whore. I'll be ownin' this farm by year's end, and ye'll be cleanin' me piss up with your tongue!"

"You think I am here alone, and there are no witnesses to what you tried to do? What made you think you could just ride up here and rape me as if it was normal business? You are lucky my son did not kill you. My husband will be back soon, and you can ride back to Ireland with your sheep for all I care," Heidi snarled at him, her shoulder stinging now. She could feel the warm blood trickle down her back and side.

Tor finally came up the lane driving the empty wagon pulled by a team of horses. He hurried when he saw the big black horse tethered to his hitching rail. "What on earth happened here?" he questioned when he saw Esus tied to the post. The man had dried blood in his mustache below a red and swollen nose. He looked at Heidi and saw the blood caked on her shoulder and down her dress. He jumped down from the wagon, strode up, looking at the ground where the struggle took place.

"Apparently, Esus here feels that I am included in the price for the sheep," she said calmly, as if she felt no pain.

"I come up here askin' for a bit o' tea, an' your sprout whacks me over the 'ead wi' a club. Ye need to be teachin' your heathen family some manners. But I 'spect ye'll all learn at the Althing come midsummer then, won't ye?" Esus growled.

"What happened?" Tor looked to Heidi.

She told him, in detail, all that had transpired. How Esus had her in a bad place and Erik sneaked up and knocked him out with a piece of firewood.

"Esus, I have known this woman many years.

One thing I do know about her is that she does not lie. She has more protection under Icelandic Law than you do. I will untie you now, but you will ride back to the dock, bound as you are now, in my wagon, while my wife rides your horse. You will take your sheep back to Ireland and not return to Borg ever again. Is that clear?" Tor addressed Esus as a father would, though they were about the same age.

"Ye'll see me again at the Althing, and I'll be ownin' this parcel o' ground," Esus snapped back.

"Then I will just leave you tied up here until you come to your senses. If that does not happen by morning, I will leave you right there, tied up as you are until I can fetch the gothi of this district, and we'll make the ruling on your complaint before you are turned loose. How does that sound?"

"Ye can't do that."

"Oh, I can, and I will. What's it going to be?"

"Turn me loose, I'll be gone." Esus spoke in a low voice as he looked at the ground.

That night, as she lay awake, Heidi whispered into the darkness, "Wolf, can you hear me? Tell me, friend, is this how it always will be? Will I always be tested?"

Taking the lesson, Heidi endeavored to get herself in fighting condition and stay that way as long as she could. With Cairenn to help with the children and chores, Heidi soon was able to do more work than most men. Her training routine soon had her wielding weapons like a fabled shield maiden.

CHAPTER 7

BATTLE

Ten days prior to the summer solstice two years later, three longships pulled up to the docks below Borg. Their reason for docking in Borg was to recruit warriors to sail for the Mediterranean Sea to pillage and trade for exotic treasure and goods. The ships had come from Norway by way of Dublin, where they found four warriors willing to partake in the dangerous voyage. One had been to Borg before, and he had a score to settle.

In the ale house near the docks, Ferrminn Homallarsson sat at a small table drowning his sorrows, as usual, when Thorm Bjarnisson, leading five warriors from the newly arrived longships, walked into the room. Thorm announced he was there to recruit brave men for a great voyage that would result in much wealth and glory for any man willing to take the risks. Thorm looked at Ferrminn and thought he had a warm body to fill a rowing bench.

"What about you? From the looks of you, a glorious voyage is just what you need."

"I would be willing, but I have a problem here that needs to be solved first." Ferrminn looked up at Thorm with pleading eyes.

"I care nothing of your local problems. I need warriors." Thorm stood with his fists resting on his hips as he glared at Ferrminn.

"It is Tor Eriksson. I need to deal with him first." Ferrminn looked at his half-empty horn of ale and slumped his shoulders.

"What did you say?" Memories of an embarrassing defeat flooded into Thorm's head.

"Tor Eriksson, I must rid the world of him."

"Who is this Tor Eriksson?"

"He owns a big sheep farm north of this village. He is stealing all of my trade. And he has a Skræling whore in his bed. That cannot be permitted in this land! He should be banned from being a landman."

"Why do you not just go out there and kill him?"

"He is too crafty, and his woman is a witch and sorceress. Dark powers are beckoned at her will."

"That is crazy talk. Where is this Tor Eriksson from?" Thorm was thinking Tor could be his old rival from Ulfrstadt. It would be a pleasure cutting him down. But he was reported missing several years past.

"He claims he was on a ship that ran into storms that pushed him into the heart of Vinland where he alone survived the shipwreck. He supposedly grew to be a man there before finding a way back to these shores. He brought that whore with him and has five half-breed brats with her. They are evil, I say. But there has been no legal challenge and they are allowed in our midst. They must be stopped."

"And you want help to go out there and put a stop to this evil living on your doorstep? And after it is done, you will join our voyage to fame and glory?" Thorm was practically salivating with the idea of killing Tor Eriksson. After that, he might see what charms this Skræling sorceress might have worth using.

"Yes, I would go on your voyage if I could eliminate Tor Eriksson." Ferrminn was suddenly smiling and could see clearly for the first time in years. He knew of Heidi's beauty and thought she would make a great thrall on his farm and in his bed.

By midmorning the next day, twenty-three men assembled before Tor's hall. All but one wore chain mail tunics, helmets, wielded swords, or battle axes, and carried shields. One stood in the back, wearing a dark-gray leather tunic and carried a long bow and quiver of iron-tipped arrows. To his side was a smoking pot with hot tar and a bucket with six arrows with wool cloth wrapped around iron points that could be dipped into the hot tar and shot into the flammable parts of the hall.

Tor and Egill stood in front of the hall. They were also wearing chain mail tunics and carried swords and shields. Only Egill wore a helmet. Unseen in the shadows to the side of the hall was Heidi wearing a leather dress, holding her strung bow, and carrying a quiver of iron-tipped arrows.

Thorm led the warriors and stood in front of the others. A step back to his right was Ferrminn Homallarsson. Next to him stood the Irishman, Esus. Three more Irishmen were behind Esus.

"What is it you have come to this hall to do?" Tor called out so that all the men who stood before him could hear.

"We have come to rid this district of Skræling scum and dimwitted cowards." Thorm pounded on his shield with the hilt of his sword. Soon, all the men were beating on their shields and chanting, "Kill!"

Tor held his hands out to his side, palms up, and waited for the noise to settle down.

"Up to your old tricks, Thorm? I thought we settled that many years past. I understand you are in Iceland to recruit warriors for a great voyage. I suggest you go about that business and leave me and my family alone. We are not interested in glory or stolen wealth.

"All you men, Thorm has brought you here so that you could defeat me, something he was unable to do when we were young. This fight has nothing to do with you or your great voyage in quest of riches and fame. Yes, you could easily kill me and sack this farm. Is there great glory in killing a sheep farmer? You must ask yourselves, 'What am I doing here?' Realize that Thorm is here on a personal vendetta that will get some of you hurt, and there will be no wealth or glory gained. Think about that."

Tor stood his ground and waited for his words to settle on the men before him. He noted some murmuring between warriors.

"Spoken like the coward he is!" Thorm called out.

"Ah, there may be no glory, but I know there be a handsome lass worth a bruise or two on this farm." Esus spoke up.

"Do not delude yourself into thinking you could take her alive, Esus. She would not be so kind to you a second time." Tor spoke with confidence.

Thorfein Grimmsson of Ulfrstadt spoke out, "I knew the family of Erik Haraldsson, and Tor Eriksson as a child in Ulfrstadt. They were an honorable lot. I hold no grudge against this man. His words are true. This fight is not ours, and I will not stand and watch this foolishness. All who will follow me can return to our ship with confidence we did the right thing." He sheathed his sword and turned to the road back to Borg. All but the lone archer, Ferrminn, Thorm, Esus, and his three followers followed Thorfein.

With hate in his eyes, Thorm raised his sword.

The bowman started to raise his bow and draw his arrow back. Before his bow was fully drawn, an arrow flew from the side of the hall. With his concentration on Tor's chest, the archer did not see the arrow slicing the air in his direction until it was too late to avoid. The arrow drove deep into his chest, punching out his back with a burst of blood, muscle, lung matter, and air. He dropped and lay on the ground in disbelief, trying to breathe while frothy blood filled his mouth.

Thorm strode toward Tor, pulling his shield up higher and brandishing his sword. Ferrminn slowly retreated toward the warriors who followed Thorfein. Esus followed Thorm in his attack on Tor. His men were right behind him. Egill advanced to intercept Esus.

Heidi's next arrow hit one of the Irishmen in the neck before he had his shield up. He was dead before his body crumpled to the ground. Seeing the attack from the side, another Irishman raised his sword and started for Heidi.

Gorm's first swing hit Tor's shield with a loud "thwack" and splintering of wood. Tor's counter caught Gorm on the thick chain mail and leather sword belt covering his hip. The blow knocked Gorm off balance but did little damage.

Egill rammed his shield into that of Esus so hard, the Irishman tumbled backward into the last of his warriors, who was trying to advance on Tor.

Tor attacked the faltering Thorm with hard blows to his shield, splintering wood with each slam. Thorm finally twisted away, out of Tor's reach.

Egill advanced on Esus while he and his warrior were entangled. Egill's swing was parried by the warrior as Esus recovered his balance. Seeing an opening, Esus thrust his sword up into Egill's armpit. Somehow, the sword missed any arteries as the blade pierced into muscle. Egill's arm dropped, the hilt of his sword striking Esus just below his helmet, hitting him in the eye, temporarily blinding him. That gave Egill a chance to back away from the entangled Irishmen, but he knew he was out of the fight.

The Irishman who went after Heidi was coming too quickly for her to nock another arrow and shoot, so she cast her bow aside and grabbed her axe from her belt. The warrior was on her before she could plan an attack of her own. She sidestepped his brutal sword swing, but she saw the long weapon was still going to hit her. Instinctively, she threw her hip into the impact. By luck alone, the attacker's sword tip slammed into the quiver that still held twelve arrows. The leather case and wooden arrows absorbed the impact of the strike, and she was able to counter with her axe just under his shield. Her axe cut deeply into his thigh, causing severe damage to his leg. He went down hard, spewing blood in all directions. She looked around and saw that Tor was about to be overwhelmed by Thorm, Esus, and his friend.

Heidi determined she could not get to his attackers before they got to Tor. She put everything she had into throwing her axe at Esus. Esus, intent on driving his sword into Tor's side, and his left eye swollen half-shut, did not see the axe speeding at him until just before it struck. His eyes widened, but he was not able to avoid the sharp blade of the axe just before it struck him square in the face. The momentum drove the heavy weapon and sharp edge through his facial bones into his brain. In a flood of blood pouring from his ruined face, he was dead before he hit the ground. His Irish companion looked down at him in horror, even as Tor's sword came from the other side and struck him in the side of his rib cage. He dropped to the ground with a lethal gash in his left side.

Tor turned his attention back to Thorm, who

had regained his feet after Tor's last assault had left him on the ground. With hate in his eyes, Thorm rushed to attack Tor once again. The battle was now reduced to Thorm against Tor. All the other warriors, including Ferrminn had fled or were out of action due to injuries or death.

Again, Thorm led with his battered shield while he tried to swing his sword beneath Tor's shield. Tor recognized Thorm's strategy, parried his sword attack, and deflected his shield away. While Thorm flailed to regain control, Tor delivered a crushing blow with his sword to Thorm's shield-side shoulder. Thorm bellowed in pain, knowing he was defeated. Tor stood tall, knowing his family had successfully defended their home.

Cairenn and Heidi tended to Egill's damaged arm while Tor got a team of horses hooked up to a wagon. He then gathered all the discarded weapons. He loaded them all on the wagon, and Heidi came to help him load the dead bodies. Finally, Tor assisted a somber Thorm, with his crippled shoulder onto the wagon. Tor sent Heidi back to help Cairenn as he drove the wagon back to Borg to get rid of his unwanted visitors.

Thorm never spoke, even as the other warriors unloaded the wagon for Tor. Thorfein told Tor that he was happy that Tor was able to defend his home, property, and life. He would spread the word in Ulfrstadt that an honorable Tor Eriksson lives in Iceland, even though none of his family is alive to hear the news.

"Bright Moon, I believe Wolf still protects you and will until the end of your days." Tor used the Monongahela tongue as he wrapped blood spattered arms around his tearful wife.

"Yes," she whispered as her only response.

CHAPTER 8
ALTHING

In the aftermath of the fight at Rolfcarllandstedr, Ferrimm Homallarsson brought charges against Tor Eriksson for manslaughter. He brought his case to Gothi Vagr Starkathr, 3rd Gothi in the Western District and got the case past the Thorsnes Thing the following spring. The case would be decided at the Althing at Thingvalr at midsummer.

When Tor learned of the charges brought against him, he was shocked. Then he learned that he was not the only defendant. Heidi and Egill were also charged with murder and assault on the day they defended their home from Thorm Bjarnisson's attack. After Tor and Heidi took bodies and all the weapons back to the dock and helped

Thorm get attention for his broken shoulder, the survivors of the raiding party set sail for Ireland. Tor considered the incident behind them and went about his business of raising sheep, horses, and children.

Tor's first reaction was to beat the messenger who brought the notice of the charges to his farm. Heidi talked him down and directed his rage to defending his honor in the courts.

Tor's second surprise was when Gothi Vagr Starkathr presented Ferrimm Homallrsson's case at the Thorsnes Thing. Tor was not prepared, thinking he only needed to tell the truth before the local gothar. Gothi Vagr presented an organized argument that left the matter undecided. That inaction sent the case to the Althing in Thingvalr at midsummer. Tor was further advised by the court to bring the other defendants and any witnesses he might find useful to his cause.

Tor went to see an aging Gothi Garmr Hallrs-son. Garmr was convinced that Tor was telling the truth and enthusiastically agreed to present his case at the Althing. Garmr told Tor that Vagr was a young farmer who was appointed gothi to get some younger people in the court system. The feeling was that the older gothi were just not up to the challenges of modern times. Garmr was the oldest gothi in the Western District, and he felt he knew the laws better than the upstart Vagr.

In the weeks between the Thorsnes Thing and the Althing, Tor, Heidi, and Egill spent much time at Garmr's hall going over the events of the attack and planning Garmr's defense. Garmr brought his two Thingmen in for the discussions and occasionally brought in another gothi for legal advice. Garmr thought his case for Tor, Heidi, and Egill's defense was very strong by the time they left for Thingvalr.

The journey to the Althing would take four or five days with two wagons loaded with all the children, their tents, bedding, cooking tools, food, etc. Fully one-third of one wagon carried stacked bricks of peat for cooking and warmth for the cool night hours, although the sun did not fully set. Heidi found the journey wonderous with the natural beauty of the land and wide -open vistas.

"It is like my homeland without the tress," Heidi told everyone.

"They tell me these hills and valleys were covered with forests when the first settlers arrived. All the trees have been used for buildings and fires since the early days. Now, just a few isolated pockets of brush and small trees remain," Tor replied.

"I suppose it has been necessary but 'tis a shame to see our mother's beauty destroyed for our greed," said Cairenn.

"Well, you and I are free people and have more wealth than we ever dreamed of because this land has been tamed from the wilderness it once was. So, I think we should be thankful for it," Egill interjected.

"It is still very beautiful," Heidi said.

Tor had butchered a cow and smoked the meat before they left, and each night they enjoyed a full meal before bedding down. The wagon road to Thingvalr was well-traveled and easy to follow. It seemed everyone in the district was going to the Althing, so there were many people sharing the route. Tor noted that the people he did not know were much friendlier than those from Borg and the surrounding area. He concluded that the strangers could not tell Heidi was not Norse and held no animosity toward her and her children. That thought saddened him.

The weather was sunny and the days the warmest of the year so far. The nights barely dimmed the sun as it lowered toward the northwestern hills but did not fully set. The short nights made it difficult to get the children to sleep. The twins and Unndis were too excited until their little bodies ran out of energy. Then they were irritable and hard to deal with. Cairenn helped Heidi all she could, but her own toddler was difficult enough for the young mother. Erik, Gerna, and Heidi Egillsdottir helped some, but they needed sleep, too. They walked along beside the wagons to lighten the load for the horses and were exhausted when it came time to stop for the night.

When their wagons topped the hill that led into the final leg of their journey, Heidi looked on in awe. The wide valley opened with a small river winding its way toward a long lake. The hills sloped gently up the sides, then became steep until they reached a ridge on the east and west sides. Past the east ridge, steam and smoke rose in wisps.

"Is the volcano you told me about over that ridge, Father?" Erik asked.

"Yes, I believe so, son."

"Can we go look at it?"

"Maybe, but I will need to talk to someone to see if it is safe to travel over there. We will be here for two weeks. You will need to be patient," said Tor.

"It is like Cahokia!" Heidi exclaimed as the wagons started down the slope into Thingvalr. Hundreds of tents covering the open ground were set aside for personal use. Hundreds of people milled around the tents and formal speaking sites set up for the Althing. A group of sod houses were set off to the side of the lake away from the tent areas. These were the houses that would shelter the important gothi during the two-week event.

"Like Cahokia, except here the hills are not manmade," Tor replied. Looking closely, he noted an area set up that had a place for a speaker, then seats that fanned out in three rows around the speaker's place, like an amphitheater. *Logretta, it is the site where the gothar will listen to the law speaker and make policy decisions. If I learned it correctly, each gothi will sit in the middle chair with one thingman in front and one behind him.*

Back from the river a couple hundred paces, Heidi noticed a steeper valley coming in from the east side. A large rock feature that had a distinct trail winding up around the back side to the top stood prominently in the north wall of that side valley.

Tor pointed to the rock and said, "There is the *logberg* or Law Rock. The law speaker will open the

Althing from there. He will also recite one-third of the laws passed to date by the gothar, any new laws, and important decisions made by the gothar and the courts during the Althing."

"Will our case be announced to the whole country?" Heidi asked.

"Yes, I presume it will, my wife. No time to be shy, I expect!" Tor answered her.

"We need to find a place in this crowd where we can set up our camp," Heidi said, as she scanned the packed tent city.

"Over on that western fringe is the most level open place I can see," Tor replied. "Now, I need to find a path to get us there!"

Tor slowly maneuvered the wagon around the crowded tent city until he made it to the site he planned. Egill and his family arrived a bit later after being delayed by people blocking his path from time to time. When Tor finally stopped, a man who had bought sheep from him greeted and welcomed his family to camp next to them. The families pitched in, and by the time Egill arrived, the tents were set up and a suitable firepit dug. The cooking equipment, peat, and food were in Egill's wagon. Heidi and Cairenn, with help from Gerna and Cairenn's daughter, Heidi, helped prepare a meal for the travelers.

The men discussed the sheer size of the Althing and how so many people could come together in peace. Looking around, they did not notice any arguments involving weapons. Sure, some were bickering about some minor infraction or another, but no fists were flying, no one was wrestling on the ground, and no weapons were being wielded.

"Word has it you have been accused of murder and must stand before the court. That surprises me. I thought you were a peaceful man," Berghof Haldunsson, the sheep buyer, said.

"I hope the court finds that my actions were defensive, Berghof. My family was attacked by a group led by men with old grudges. We defended ourselves. That should have ended the story. But a jealous sheep farmer, who was in on the attack, decided he would press charges," Tor replied.

"Ah, Ferrminn Homallarsson. He is spreading the word about your evil deeds. His story is full of holes and changes with each telling, depending how long he has been at the ale house. I pray you are freed of the charges, and he is punished for telling falsehoods. It is hard to believe that Vagr

Starkathr listened and got it through the Thornes Thing Court," Berghof said.

"They are all envious of Heidi's beauty and just want Tor out of the way." Egill snickered. All three laughed, but Tor secretly wondered if the real reason they wanted him out of the way was to make Heidi a slave to be abused by any Norseman who wanted her.

Around midmorning the next day a large crowd had gathered at the Law Rock. Thorkell Tjorvason stood at the precipice and addressed the gathered throngs. The steep walls of the valley helped project his voice so that much of the crowd could hear him.

"People of the Free State of Iceland, the time has come to open this annual meeting. It is my privilege to announce the opening of the Icelandic Althing! This event is made possible by your compassion for freedom and willingness to work together to solve any issues before us in a way that makes us the freest country in all of Europe and, to my knowledge, all of the world. No where else on God's green earth are men so empowered to settle their differences. For that, we Icelanders have earned the right to be proud.

"We have much business to be conducted

before we get to the games and fun part of the Althing. In one hour, I will begin reciting the one-third of the laws passed by previous Gothar. Over the next few days, the full Gothar will meet to resolve any new laws or clarifications of old ones. After that, there will be court sessions for disputes from each quarter. When those are resolved, the Gothar will meet again to finalize the courts' decisions. I will then announce those decisions right here. Once that is done, we will proceed to the competitions. Good luck to all, have a cup of mead, and come back here in an hour to hear the laws recited." The Law Speaker concluded and turned away from the steep cliff.

The rest of that day featured the Law Speaker reciting laws passed by previous Gothar, with breaks for midday and evening meals. When the Law Speaker finished his recitations, the sun was still a good distance from the northwestern horizon. It would not slip out of view for the duration of the midsummer celebration.

CHAPTER 9
TRIAL

Thorkell Tjorvason took a special interest in the court session where Tor Eriksson was accused of murder. Tor's history intrigued the Law Speaker to the point where he took the role of announcing the court session, introducing the thirty-six judges and the advocates for each side of the dispute to the court and spectators.

The rules allowed the speaker for each side of the dispute to give statements and call witnesses. Each of the judges could ask questions and make comments. Likewise, the Law Speaker could speak for or against either side and question witnesses. No one else was permitted to speak during the proceeding.

The judges were seated in the ring of chairs where the Gothar sat for their sessions. The advocates, Law Speaker, accuser, accused, and witnesses were seated in the middle of the ring; the accuser group to one side and the accused group to the other side.

When the judges and participants were all seated, the Law Speaker stood and began his introduction.

"This court of the Althing will come to order. The court will decide the guilt or innocence of the accused and hand out any penalties assessed. Spectators will remain quiet during the entire proceeding. Today the court will hear from the accuser, Ferrminn Homallarsson. Ferrminn charges that on June the fourteenth of last year, Tor Eriksson murdered one man and assaulted two others with a sword, Heidr Tungl Torswife murdered three men, and Egill Hallundsson attempted to murder one man and assaulted two others. Further, Tor Eriksson is accused of being an impostor, having induced Thorkell Rolfcarlsson into handing over his large farm, bringing an unwed Skræling into Iceland, and producing offspring with the whore. These are Ferrminn's words. This is the nature of this court session," Law Speaker said.

He then went on to introduce all of the participants and witnesses. Ferrminn was astonished to see Bergi Baldrsson, keeper of the ale house, on the accused side of the seating. When the participants were all pointed out, Thorkell introduced each judge and told which quarter and district he hailed from.

When the introductions were complete, the Law Speaker told Gothi Vagr Starkathr he could begin with accusations.

Vagr stood and methodically made eye contact with each judge before he began. "Great men of this court, you are here to listen to testimony concerning one of the evilest men to ever set a foot on Iceland's hallowed soil. This man came to this island, found one of our beloved elders, Thorkell Rolfcarlsson, and courted the aging man's good nature until he convinced the old man that he was the long-lost nephew, the sole survivor of two ships everyone knows went down in a terrible storm just off the coast of this island. Any man with knowledge of the sea knows that surviving in these freezing waters is impossible. And we also know that no Norseman would last ten years among the Skræling of Vinland, as this villain"—he pointed a finger at Tor— "convinced the ailing Thorkell.

"So, to begin with, we are dealing with an unscrupulous liar and thief. Then, he drags a Skræling thrall from who-knows-where into Thorkell's hall and convinces him she is his wife!" A pause with Vagr's lips bent in a sardonic grin.

"So, we cannot be surprised when we learn that a group of honorable men, one of whom knew Tor Eriksson in Norway, went to the farm to confront this evil man. Tor Eriksson had laid a deadly trap for them and murdered, with the help of the Vinland witch and the ne'er-do-well, Egill Hallundsson, six men and severely injured two others. These victims were attacked without warning or provocation. They were engaged in performing a civic duty and faced death as their reward.

"I wish to call Ferrminn Homallarsson to testify," Vagr finished his opening statement.

Ferrminn stepped up to Vagr with eyes darting from judge to judge, Tor, Heidi, and everyone else, except Vagr.

Vagr put a gentle hand on Ferrminn's shoulder and asked, "Did I speak the truth about Tor Eriksson and the others?"

"You did," Ferrminn replied.

"I am finished with this witness and have no other witnesses, Speaker Thorkell, as all other witnesses are dead or have sailed from this land. You may return to your seat, Ferrminn," Vagr said confidently, a grin on his face.

"I would reserve the right to question this witness a bit later," Gothi Garmr Hallrsson said as he stood and walked to the center.

"That would be permissible, Gothi Garmr," the Law Speaker replied.

"Thank you, Speaker. Judges." Garmr spread his arms to take in all thirty-six judges. "You have been told a story of an evil man with power and wealth as his only friends. I would start by saying that a story is exactly what it is. Tor Eriksson has survived a life of remarkable events. I have spent much time with him and can testify that he is no liar. He did survive a harrowing voyage that left him, a boy of twelve winters, alone on a beach in a foreign land that none of us can imagine.

"But survive he did. And grew up among the

people of that land, met his remarkable wife, and continued to travel in what we call Vinland. His telling depicts Vinland larger than all of Europe, with many nations spread across it. At some point, he learned of Norsemen trading cloth for trees in one of the many fjords on the coast. The ship he found was owned by Thorkell Rolfcarlsson, Tor's great-uncle on his father's side. That ship brought Tor and his wife to Iceland. At that time, the couple had a son, and she was with their second child. They now have five children.

"A year ago, three ships showed up at Borgarnes. They were there to recruit warriors for a daring raid in the Mediterranean Sea. A rather odd enterprise, I thought, since most Norse warriors were busy keeping English armies at bay in Wessex. At any rate, a squad went into Bergi Baldersson's Ale Haus looking for desperate men. They found Ferrminn Homallarsson, who had a grievance against Tor Eriksson. The leader of the squad had known Tor when they were boys and considered him an enemy. Thorm Bjarnisson gladly recruited some shipmates to solve Ferrminn's problem. A small army showed up at Tor's hall the next morning. The intent was to either frighten Tor from his farm or kill him outright.

"Tor apparently gave a speech that convinced most of the warriors to abandon the fight with him. Those who insisted on fighting learned they were up against better warriors and suffered greatly for their effort.

"Therefore, this fight was self-defense on Tor and his family's part. And, as far as Tor being the rightful owner of Rolfcarllandstedr, I have, in my possession, proof that Thorkell wanted Tor to own the farm after his demise. And that was before Thorkell became feeble. Tor's identity is not in question, and any killings were self-defense. I suggest these charges against Tor Eriksson, Heidr Tungl Torswife, and Egill Hallundsson be dropped," Gothi Garmr concluded his statement.

"What about the Skræling whore and half-breed brats?" Ferrminn asked.

"What about them?" the Law Speaker cut in. "There is no law that forbids a man from taking a wife in his travels. And she has converted to Christianity, so there is no issue with the church or the state," the Law Speaker replied.

"There should be!" Ferrminn groused.

"So, you swallow this impossible story that Tor

has been to the heart of a vast Vinland, survived and come back as if he was a nobleman all along?" Gothi Vagr asked Gothi Garmr.

"No evidence has come to light that casts doubt on his story. Like I said, Thorkell Rolfcarlsson gave me indisputable proof that Tor is his deceased brother's grandson. His brother was Jarl Harald Rolfcarlsson of Ulfrland in Norway. That would make him nobility." Gothi Garmr spoke with no emotion in his voice.

"You fed me a bundle of lies, didn't you?" Gothi Vagr said sharply to Ferrminn.

"H-he stole my trade," Ferrminn snapped.

"You squandered your trade sipping ale and mead in my ale house all afternoon nearly every day," Bergi interjected.

The lead judge spoke up. "We have heard enough! The charges against Tor Eriksson, Heidr Tungl Torswife, and Egill Hallundsson are hereby dropped. Gothi Vagr, we will recommend to the Gothar that you be replaced as a local gothi and never be given a seat on the Althing Gothar. You listened to this man's lies and did nothing to verify anything he told you. That is on you!"

Everyone started to get up and move away from the circle. From somewhere in the crowd of spectators came, "Skræling lover!" "This is not over, Eriksson!" "I want a piece of that brown whore!" and several other assorted insults to Tor, Heidi, and Egill.

"Those people who do not think for themselves will always be led the wrong way," Gothi Garmr said.

As they made their way back to their camp, most people gave positive support to Heidi and Tor. A few insults continued to float in from the crowds, but none that could be clearly identified with any individuals.

Erik, Gerna, and Cairenn's Heidi wanted to watch and compete in some of the games, swim in the warm waters at the far end of the lake, and go see the volcano for themselves. The families stayed until their children were finished with their activities before packing up and moving back to Rolfcarllandstedr.

Their view of the volcano was limited to the top of the ridge where they could look down on the plain with the active eruption. The volcano featured a long slit in the land. Red, molten rock could be seen frothing into the air along that slit. Globs of the boiling rock spattered some distance from the slit, prohibiting any closer inspection.

Steam and dark-brown smoke hissed and billowed from the slit as the molten rock shot into the air. The breeze carried the smoke and steam away from their overlook, so they did not experience the strong sulfur odor from the eruption.

ICELAND

CHAPTER 10
BULLIES

Upon returning to the farm, there was much work to be done. All of their flocks that had been running free for three weeks needed to be reacquainted with their human caretakers. Some needed grooming and combing to extract wool fibers from their thick coats. Those fibers needed to be cleaned and spun onto spools to make various fabrics. A few sheep needed to be slaughtered to fill larders before the coming winter.

The horses all needed to be groomed and worked with to get used to their humans again. Heidi was the best horse talker on the farm. She had an innate ability to work with each horse that no one else could match. Egill thought he could handle any horse, but Heidi got better results, much faster than Egill could. She never disciplined them, only praised and rewarded them for good behavior. Even the wildest stallions responded to her methods quickly. Tor and Egill were in awe of Tor's wife. And now, nine-year-old Gerna was showing her mother's aptitude with horses.

"Erik, I am sending you to Borg tomorrow with six sheep to place in the market. I want you to get the best price you can get. Take payment only in silver but don't haggle until you lose the sale. Just get what you can. The important thing is you start learning how the process works."

"Yes, Father. I have watched you many times. I think I know what to do," Erik said with confidence.

"Good. Egill and I need to go to the northern fields to sort the flocks up there and bring back more for market and slaughter."

"Can I go with Erik, Father? I want to learn the market, too," Gerna pleaded.

"Erik is eleven and you will not be ten until midwinter. Are you sure you are ready?" Tor looked to Heidi to gauge her reaction.

"Of course I am ready. I can do anything Erik can do," Gerna exclaimed.

Tor kept his eyes on Heidi. She smiled and shrugged her shoulders as if saying, "Your call."

"I guess it can't hurt, as long as you do not fight with one another and come straight home after the sheep are sold. You should be home by midday before your mother starts to worry." Again, Tor looked at Heidi for reaction.

"Yes, I will expect both of you home and cleaned up for midday meal," Heidi said in support of Tor's decision to let Gerna help Erik with the trip to market.

The days were still long, with only a short period of darkness each night, although that dark period was getting noticeably longer as the season moved along. Erik and Gerna used the long daylight to get the "cage" wagon ready to leave in the morning. Gerna cleaned any old bedding and manure left in the wooden cage that sat on a flat wagon bed. Then, she put in fresh hay bedding for the two-hour trip to the Borg marketplace. Erik made sure the wheels turned freely and were solidly attached to the axels. He made sure the harness and hardware were all in working order.

In the morning, they would bring the sheep from a holding pen and herd them into the wagon that would be backed up to a ramp made for the purpose of loading sheep into wagons. When the sheep were loaded and the gate closed on the wagon, a single horse would be brought around and backed into the leather, wood, and chain traces. The leather straps attached a length of wood on each side of the horse. Iron chains attached the wood members to the ends of the front axle. Erik and Gerna walked alongside the horse and guided it down the path toward Borg. The cart track was relatively flat with a very gentle slope, making an easy walk for the sturdy horse, two children, and their trained sheep dog, Freyja.

The market was bustling by the time they arrived, but Erik knew where to bring the wagon. The workers directed Erik to the unloading ramp where they had to wait their turn to show their sheep. In the market, there were horses, cattle, sheep, goats, and pigs for sale. Fowl were sold in a separate arena. In the holding area where Erik and Gerna waited to be called, there were a few other sheep dogs that did not necessarily get along with one another. Gerna had to keep a tight grip on Freyja to keep her out of a biting, snarling fracas.

Within an hour, they called on Erik to unload his sheep. With Gerna's help, he backed the wagon up to the ramp. Gerna took Freyja into the arena and waited for Erik to open the wagon gate. The crowd of men there to buy livestock smiled in anticipation of the clown show the two kids would put on selling their sheep.

When Erik opened the gate, an explosion of baaing sheep burst into the arena and started to scatter. Gerna nudged Freyja with her leg, and the dog went to work. Within a minute, the dog had the six sheep gathered into a tight group in front of the saleclerk's stand. The crowd hushed instantly and marveled at the dog's skill. Not that they had not seen good dogs working sheep in the arena. Just not one handled by a child.

From a few places around the crowd looking over the sheep came a few jeers. "It's those half-breed Skræling kids!" "I would not buy a thing from those half animals!" "Get them out of here so decent men can buy decent sheep!"

The man running the market yelled out, "Those sheep come from Tor Eriksson's flocks, they are the finest sheep in western Iceland. These are six shorn wethers. Who cares to offer a bid?"

At an unheard command from Gerna, Freyja herded the sheep into a single line and paraded them around the arena so that all could look at them. Soon, bids started to trickle in. Each bid upped the price.

Before long, the bid was up to a whole eyrir for the lot, a better price than Erik hoped for. When the sale was settled, Erik put the coin in his breast pocket. Soon, Erik, Gerna, and Freyja were leading the horse and wagon back toward home and feeling pretty good about their morning.

As they made their way toward home, they reached a lonely stretch of the cart track. On one side was a small gully along the side of the road. To the other side was a picturesque wide valley that led off to the southwest. At a certain point, the sea was in sight. Erik and Gerna were marveling at the beauty when a young man's voice sounded from behind them.

"Look what we have here! A pair of Skræling half-breeds. Maybe they don't know the way of the world and need some lessons, eh, Grimhald?" A young man Erik did not recognize spoke in a sharply sarcastic tone. But there were five boys in the group, and all were a year or two older than Erik.

"What is it you want?" Erik asked with caution.

"First, I want that silver coin in your pocket.

Then I think my friends and I want to have a go at your sister. If you object, I would like to bloody your face. You see, your kind are useless thieves. You do not deserve that coin, so give it over to a real Norseman." He held his hand out toward Erik with his palm up, as if Erik would hand the coin over on his demand.

Unthinking, Erik put his hand to his breast pocket and felt to make sure the coin was still there. "I think I will keep it," Erik said matter-of-factly.

Grimhald started toward Erik with his fist knotted. "I will teach you, you little worm!" he grunted as he advanced.

"I will handle him," said Haldor Tammersson, the apparent leader. The three other boys just stayed back and flashed eyes back and forth between Erik and Haldor.

"You should think twice about giving me that coin," Haldor said to Erik.

"And I think you should leave me and my sister alone," Erik replied.

"Mistake!" called Haldor as he charged at Erik with fists balled and ready to strike.

Erik deftly sidestepped Haldor's charge and tripped him with a fast kick to the shin as he went by. Haldor went down in the dirt and came up with hate in his gray eyes. He charged again, trying to connect with a roundhouse punch to Erik's head.

Erik ducked the punch and delivered a hard fist to Haldor's chest. Stunned, unable to breathe, Haldor dropped to his knees.

Seeing his idol hurt, Grimhald charged Erik, who had his back turned. Erik felt the impact as the bigger and heavier boy tackled him. They went down in a heap and Erik quickly felt a fist slam into his back. Acting on instinct from the fight training Tor had given him, Erik tucked his shoulder into the dirt of the cart track and threw all his strength into rolling over and pushing the bigger boy off him with his legs. It worked, and Erik quickly took advantage of his superior position and drove a fist into the side of Grimhald's rib cage. The boy was momentarily stunned. Erik hit his adversary in the back of the head as hard as he could. Grimhald fell limp, face down of the cart track.

Erik looked up to see Haldor had recovered and was coming after him. Erik worried about the other three, but quickly noted that Freyja and Gerna had them cowering in the ditch, afraid to move, lest the vicious, snarling dog would tear them apart.

Erik turned to Haldor, who was closing fast. Erik dropped and rolled into Haldor's knees before the bully knew what hit him. Haldor went down again as Erik rolled past and was back on his feet before Haldor could get up.

"Stay down!" Erik demanded.

Haldor spun on his hurting knees and started to rise when Erik's right fist slammed into his face. Haldor's nose broke and blood gushed from the wreckage. With hate in his eyes, Haldor looked up at Erik, but he held up a hand and said, "No more."

"Hate is always a bad choice," Erik said, offering Haldor a hand.

"Don't touch me, half-breed," Haldor squeaked out in a nasal twang mixed with spraying blood. "Next time, you won't be so lucky. No one has ever beat me in a fight, and you won't again."

"There is no need for your hostility, Haldor. I have never seen you before, so there is no way that I have hurt you before this. Why do you hate me?" Tor asked.

Haldor just helped Grimhald, who had just rolled over, get on his feet. He was obviously disoriented and out of fight, too.

Gerna asked the others if they were finished. They just wanted the dog to leave them alone. She called Freyja off and went to Erik. "Are you well, brother?"

"I'll be sore a day or two." He flexed his swollen hands and stretched his back.

"Next time we go to Borg, I am bringing an axe," Gerna said. "Thank God our parents taught us how to defend ourselves. I almost sent Freyja to help you. I think I would have had my hands full without her." Gerna's voice was still full of adrenaline.

"Hah, Freyja was your axe today! I hope this day is never repeated." Erik kept looking behind them, but there was no pursuit.

"What happened to you two?" Heidi questioned as they came in the door late. She could see the mess that had been Erik's clothing. "Who have you been fighting and why?" she demanded.

"Some boys followed us and started calling us names. They wanted the silver coin Erik got for Father's sheep. Erik would not hand it over, so two of them attacked him. I kept the other three out of it with Freyja. She is such a good dog. In the arena, she impressed everyone. I think that is why Erik got a good price for the sheep." Gerna finally stopped her monologue.

"Who were these boys?" Heidi asked.

"I never saw any of them before. I only got two names. One was called Haldor, the other, Grimhald. We did not get any other names, and I don't know where they are from," Erik replied.

"Are the bad boys coming here, like those bad men, Mother?" young Erna asked.

"I do not think so, child. You need not worry about them," Heidi replied.

In the following days, Tor and Egill worked tirelessly with Erik to improve his self-defense abilities. Tor knew he could not be with his son at all times, and obviously the boy needed to be able to defend himself and his sisters.

"These fighting skills are only to be used to defend yourself or your family. He who starts fights is usually a coward and thinks he is superior to anyone he attacks. Make sure you are not that person. Understand?"

"Yes, Father. I have no desire to bully others, but I will defend myself, my family, and this farm," Tor said.

Heidi also spent extra time working with Gerna. She showed the girl more advanced fighting techniques using a club or an axe. She also trained Gerna on ways to damage an opponent with various kicks and punches. Finally, she sewed a secret pocket in the waistline of Gerna's pants and dresses where a small knife could be hidden.

"This is only to be used in an emergency. If some enemy gets you in a bad way, this little knife can be used to cut bindings or through something like a tent wall. It is very sharp and can inflict intense pain if used right, as well. But it is very small and should be used as a weapon of last resort," Heidi instructed.

Then Heidi showed Gerna how to get the knife out and its different uses in confined spaces. She had Gerna practice getting the knife out and free her hands when they were bound behind her back. Gerna learned quickly and became very adroit in her escape methods.

As time passed, Heidi began the same lessons with her younger daughters. By the time Unndis was in her eighth year, she was an expert fighter. Although not very big, she was quick, and Heidi had taught her where she could hurt a man or a woman the most.

CHAPTER II
TAKEN

Erik and Gerna had taken several more trips hauling sheep to market with no more incidents. They were becoming complacent, even venturing to take Erna and Gerdis when they turned nine years old. On that trip, the worst they heard from anonymous hecklers was, "Oh god, there are more of them. Please keep our families safe, Lord!"

The trip was successful, and the girls enjoyed going to town without their parents for a change. But the twins thought the trip was long and boring. Riding in a wagon with a bunch of smelly sheep was not their idea of a wondrous enterprise. They did not beg for a second adventure.

It was mid-August when Erik and Gerna made

their next trip to market. They used the bigger freight wagon, pulled by two horses. Tor and Egill had long since built a makeshift sheep pen that could be temporarily placed on the big cart. When filled, it would carry twenty-four adult sheep. On this trip, they carried twelve rams, six bred ewes, and twelve weaned lambs.

The prices were good, and the brother and sister were making the return trip by midmorning. Freyja was curled up on the box seat next to Gerna while Erik drove the wagon. He was sixteen now and had grown large and handsome. Gerna, at fourteen, was beautiful like her mother and sported an athletic body that attracted much unwanted attention. They got to that place on the trail where they could see all the way to the sea and stopped to stretch their legs a bit.

———

In a corner of the arena, a group of young men stood discussing the physical attributes of young Gerna Torsdottir.

"I would like to dip my manhood in that cookie box," Grimhald said with a sardonic grin on his face.

"You can have her!" Haldor hissed. He was missing two front teeth, and his nose was crooked from his last encounter with Erik Torsson five years past.

"Why have we waited so long? They have been coming to market for years, and she just keeps getting riper. I say we follow them and not make any mistakes this time. I am ready!"

"Because I have been working out a deal and have a plan," Haldor hissed again, keeping his voice low.

"What plan?" Grimhald asked.

"Shh! You fool. No one needs to know except me, for now. But yes, let us get up the trail to set a trap," Haldor whispered. "Halvar, Ingvar, Konur, let's go. Carry these bags like I showed you," Haldor told his other three friends.

"Why don't we take the cart trail? Wouldn't it be much easier?" Ingvar asked while they made their way north up the valley close to the road.

"Because I said to go this way. Now, shut up and ride as quietly as you can," Haldor replied.

———

WHEN THEY GOT to Haldor's ambush location, he laid out instructions. Konur would wait behind a rock within twenty paces of the road with his bow. "If the dog threatens, put an arrow in his heart. Understand?"

"Yes, gladly," Konur replied. He was the best bowman in their group, and he vividly remembered the gnashing teeth and vicious growl the last time they were confronted by Gerna's dog.

"Halvar and Ingvar, you get the bags ready to throw over their heads when Grimhald and I confront them. Just like we practiced. Is that clear?" Haldor asked the other members of his gang.

"Grimhald, as soon as Halvar has the bag over Erik's head, tackle him and get the ropes secured so he cannot move his arms. Remember, he is strong, but you are stronger. Get those ropes around him as fast as you can. I will do the same thing to Gerna. When we have them bound, we are going on a difficult trip to Glaumbeer. It will take us more than a week. But the rewards will be worth our effort!" Haldor beamed with pride.

"I thought we were going to beat the life out of Erik and have our fun with Gerna," Grimhald said.

"That was the plan, once. But I met a man

named Asgeir Caldersson, who trades in flesh. We will get a tidy sum of silver for the children of Tor Eriksson. Enough to buy all the women you can handle," Haldor answered with a big smile.

"But I want her."

"After Asgeir pays us for her, you can buy a go 'round with her. Personally, I don't want the filthy half-breed touching my manhood," Haldor replied.

About an hour before midday, Konur gave the bird whistle signal that the wagon was coming into view.

"Everyone in your places and do your job," Haldor admonished.

Erik pulled the reins and stopped the wagon. No other traffic was in sight, so they climbed down and started for the long swale that opened to a view of the sea. Before they had gone ten steps, a darkness covered Erik as the big wadmal bag dropped over his head. Before he could warn Gerna, a force hit him, knocking him down and pressing him into the ground. He struggled to get free, but felt ropes tightening around his shoulders, arms, waist, and legs. Struggling quickly became futile. Then a rope drew tight around his neck.

"Don't struggle, and I won't kill you." A

familiar voice sounded from outside his dark confinement.

"Grimhald? Did you not get enough the last time we met?" Erik asked. His throat was restricted by the rope around his neck.

Gerna was trying to struggle against the bag and ropes that constricted her movements. She started to cry out when Freyja's fighting sounds were interrupted with a painful yelp, followed by a weakening whine.

"Looks like your bitch won't be of much help this time," Haldor hissed in her ear from outside the bag she was wrapped in. Knowing she was immobile, Haldor got off her, and she heard him say, "Let us get this brute loaded into the wagon, then we'll get her in so we can be on our way."

Erik was trying to make sense of what was happening when he felt several hands picking him up and unceremoniously dropping him into the bed of the wagon. He started to ask about Gerna when he heard her struggling and complaining, then she was dropped into the wagon like was moments earlier. Seconds later, he heard the gate of the cage latch shut.

"Are you all right, sister?" Erik asked in a scratchy voice.

"I am alive, but with this rope around my neck, I don't know how long. I think they killed Freyja," she replied, her voice cracking with emotion.

"We need to stay strong. They are taking us someplace. We will find a way to escape, somehow," Erik replied, trying to sound confident.

The wagon headed east cross country toward the Nordra River. The going was rough and slow. There was no trail, so Haldor had to pick his way along between ditches, big rocks, drop-offs, and other obstacles on the terrain as they headed east.

"You are still a fool, Haldor. You know my father and mother will soon be after us," Erik taunted Haldor.

"You are the fool, Torsson. Nobody can follow a single wagon across this land. No, you will be traveling with us for a week or so, until we get to Glaumbeer," Haldor replied proudly.

"Glaumbeer? Why would you go to Glaumbeer? Father says it is smaller than Borg," Erik asked.

"Because there is a man there who will pay a good price for a Skræling thrall as strong as you. And a better price for a pretty virgin like your sister there."

"Too late, Haldor. He will hold you accountable

when you get me there, and I am not a virgin," Gerna bluffed.

Erik could not believe his ears. *How could she not be a virgin? Surely not Egill. She has never been around any other man.*

"Your bluff won't work on me, little sister. If Asgeir does not get what he wants, you will die, not me," Haldor replied confidently.

"Do you really think these horses will make it across the desert?" Erik asked Haldor.

"You better hope they do. It would really be hard walking across it with that bag tied over your body," Haldor answered quickly.

"Our mother can track an ant through a pine forest, Haldor. Are you sure you want to go through with this?" Gerna asked.

"I am not worried about your Skræling mother. She has others to think about. Your worthless hides are nothing to her. When a wolf loses her litter, she just goes into heat and has another litter. Your animal mother will do the same," he scoffed.

"Of course! I should have thought of that. Thank you for the lesson," Gerna mocked.

As the day wore on, the rough ride and sun beating down on the dark wadmal bags they were in began to take a toll on the prisoners.

"Are you going to keep us in these hot bags all day? We need water soon, or you will only have bodies to sell. I doubt the price will cover your expenses," Erik suggested to Haldor.

"We will be at the river soon. You will get cooled off there. But make the most of it. Four days without water will follow, in the near future," Haldor replied.

"I hope there is a good rocky field we can sleep in tonight. Anything will beat getting tortured bouncing around in this wagon," Gerna quipped.

"You better hope your father built this wagon strong enough to make to Glaumbeer. Like I said, walking will be most uncomfortable."

Gerna pondered the hopelessness of their situation. *What if our parents don't come? What if they cannot find us? And poor Freyja...she was innocent. Why did she have to die? If we get loose, I will kill Haldor personally.*

Erik struggled constantly to free his hands from their constraints, but his arms were tied tightly against his sides from outside the bag he was in. His arms and hands were becoming numb and useless, his legs no better. He prayed their mother and father would find their trail and catch them soon.

CHAPTER 12

THE SEARCH BEGINS

When Erik and Gerna did not show up for midday meal, Heidi became concerned. *It has been five years since they were attacked. I thought that was all over now. I know they like to stop at the place on the cart track where they can look at the sea. But they left early so they should be home by now. Of course, Tor and Egill are not in yet, and they are only working in the barn.*

She heard the latch on the door rattle and breathed a sigh of relief. She glanced at Cairenn, who was dishing stew out to the children while Heidi went to the door. It swung open, and Egill followed Tor in. They were laughing at some joke between them.

When Tor saw the worried look on Heidi's face, he gave her his full attention. "What is it?"

"Erik and Gerna are not home yet," she answered grimly.

"Do you think it is late? They are young people, easily distracted. Freyja is probably chasing a fox across the plains."

Seeing no change in her expression, he said, "All right, after a bowl of stew, I will ride down the road and look for them."

"I will go with you. I have a feeling that something bad has happened."

"Let us relax, have some food, then, if we have not seen them, we'll go get them. But there will be punishment unless they've had a problem."

Heidi looked at the floor as a tear trickled down her cheek. "Cairenn, can you keep an eye on the twins and Unndis? While we go see about Erik and Gerna?"

"What is wrong?" A pause. "Oh Heidi, you're having one of your feelings. Trust in the Lord but run along and do what you must. Egill and I can watch the girls. God help ye find 'em quickly," Cairenn answered, slipping into her old accent as the weight in Heidi's eyes began to set in.

"Father, is something wrong with Erik and

Gerna? They should be here, and Mother is worried," Unndis asked.

"No, child. Nothing is wrong. They are just at an age where they get distracted and forget to come home," Tor assured his youngest daughter.

"Erik always does what he is supposed to do," she replied.

"Well, almost always, little one."

While Tor was finishing his stew, Heidi was on her way to the barn to saddle her horse. She thought to bring an extra water bag to hang on each horse. She thought about packing some jerked meat but dismissed it.

Once they were on the cart track headed toward Borg, Heidi looked at Tor and said, "I have a very bad feeling about this. I know something is wrong."

"Now, let us not jump to any conclusions until we know something for sure."

"I already know my children are in trouble. I can feel it. If you want to dismiss me, fine. Turn your horse around and go home!" Another tear trickled down her cheek.

"No, I learned long ago not to doubt your instincts. I was just trying not to escalate the problem before we know what it is."

They rounded a bend and could see a long, straight stretch of open cart track. Heidi knew that near the end of that straight stretch was the overlook that Gerna always talked about. She also knew that was where the problem started. But her gut told her there were no answers close by.

They continued along at a steady pace silently, but Heidi was using all her willpower not to charge ahead. When they reached a few hundred paces from the overlook, they could see something laying on the side of the track.

"Oh god!" Heidi cried out as she kicked her horse into a full gallop. Tor was right behind her but could not get a clear look at what was lying at the side of the cart track.

Heidi reined in her horse and leaped off. She ran and dropped to her knees at the lifeless body of their dog. "Oh, Freyja, who did this to you? Poor girl, Gerna must be paralyzed with grief...and anger. She will kill whoever did this to you. I know —she is a lot like me. But where is she, girl?"

Heidi looked up at Tor. "Where are the children? Who did this? This is no distraction, my lord! WHERE ARE MY CHILDREN!?" she cried out, as if blaming Tor for what happened.

"We must settle our nerves and figure things

out from the tracks. Whatever it is, our wagon and horses are gone. The wagon will leave a trail we can follow. So let us get to work analyzing what happened here," Tor said sternly.

Tears flowing down her cheeks, Heidi looked at Tor with hate in her eyes. She stared hard into his eyes for several heartbeats. Then her eyes began to change. The old determination from Turtle Island was there. "I am sorry for lashing out at you, my husband. Nothing here is your fault. Yes, we must find their tracks, and follow them to Cahokia if we must."

Tor stepped over and wrapped his arms around her. "Whatever it takes, my wife, whatever it takes."

In the dirt, they found the tracks from the scuffle. They could not tell what happened, but it was obvious two people were laid out on the ground, though their forms were unusual. One was bigger and heavier, the other fought fiercely but was unable to break free. Heidi presumed that was Gerna. One person wearing boots picked her up and carried her a short distance, then walked away. But he only walked a little way, then stepped off the road.

"He put her in the wagon," Tor said. "Look,

here are the wheel tracks. The other one was Erik. It took four of them to put him in the wagon. They must have been tied up. How did someone do that to Erik? He is too strong for one person to subdue. I don't understand."

"What matters is, there were at least four of them. They somehow tied up our children, put them in our wagon, and left this place. We find that wagon, and we find our children...and probably the villains that took them," Heidi deduced.

"Look, they left the cart track and went off to the east. What is east of here, husband?" Heidi asked Tor.

"Not much. A few hours ride, there is a river. It is not much of one at that. Farther southeast is another river. Those flow together, then south-west, back to Borgarfjord. Farther east is a river that flows north. I do not know after that. But there are few settlements in the interior at all. The land dries into a desert. They say as many die crossing it as live." Tor looked unfocused to the east as he spoke.

"How far to the first river?" she asked.

He looked at the western sky. "If that is where they are headed, I think we can get there by dark. But I see storm clouds building to the southwest.

That plain between here and the river is rocky. It will be hard on the horses and the wagon. That wagon is well made, but I doubt it can make it across that desert. And I doubt the horses can either. They say it is up to six days without water. But, right now, we can move faster than they can across this plain. I think we can follow the wagon tracks easily enough. One more thing, for someone bound in that wagon, they are going to bounce around every step of the way. Their bodies will be nothing but bruises on bruises."

"Try not to make it sound so cheerful. We must find our children...fast!"

Tor and Heidi followed the wagon tracks just a little way when they found five sets of horse tracks joining them. "So, we have five men to deal with when we catch them. I wish I had brought my bow. Remember, at least one of them is carrying a bow—he used it on Freyja," Heidi said.

"More animals make them easier to follow," Tor noted.

They fell silent as they followed the trail. Often the wagon separated from the horses, as the driver sought an easier path across the rocky plain. Tor felt the driver was not very concerned about being followed.

The shadows were getting longer. Tor looked over his shoulder and saw the sun was now covered with storm clouds that were moving rapidly toward them. The days were now about eighteen hours long. They would continue getting shorter each day until the sun stayed below the horizon all day in December.

"Have your feelings changed? Do you think we are getting closer?" Tor asked Heidi.

"I am not getting a feeling of closeness yet, but I feel they are both still alive. But husband, they are in torturous pain." Tears once again welled in her black eyes.

The searchers topped a low hill and could see the river valley in the distance. "They must be planning to make the river before dark. We should catch them before they stop. But that storm could cause problems," Tor said.

"I was thinking the same. We could miss them in a heavy downpour or lose their trail. We should hurry," Heidi offered.

"We must make sure we don't lose their tracks. We will go as fast as the sign will allow."

"Hmph!" Heidi replied and started following the tracks again. They had not gone ten paces when a crack of thunder sounded too closely behind them. The horses became agitated and danced around, causing a delay while they looked for the tracks again once the horses settled down. The wind picked up, and they could smell rain closing.

The situation deteriorated rapidly as they were engulfed by the storm. Tor had an oil cloth tunic tied to his saddle, but Heidi had failed to bring hers. Tor gave her his although she was already soaked to the skin before she got covered.

The driving rain, gale-force wind, and darkened sky made it impossible to follow the wagon tracks.

"We should hunker down until this blows over," Tor shouted to Heidi.

"I know, but the children..." she replied, unable to finish.

—————

THEY HAD JUST REACHED the small river when the storm unleashed its fury. Haldor pulled the wagon up to a clump of birch brush close to the river. The riders were working extra hard to keep their horses under control. Once they got the horses tied off to some small willow trees, they scurried under the wagon for protection.

"What about them?" Grimhald point upward, indicating Erik and Gerna in their soaking wool cocoons in the bed of the wagon.

"Drag them down here, but don't loosen their bindings until I say to," Haldor replied.

Gerna went from near heat stroke to shivering cold in seconds. Her quivering muscles made it difficult for Haldor's friends to hold on to her. In fact, when Grimhald handed her down to Halvar and Ingvar, they dropped her on the gravelly ground, causing her to cry out in pain.

"My god, I promise if you idiots hurt my sister, I will rip your heads off!" Erik yelled out from where he lay in the wagon.

Grimhald kicked him hard in the back, grabbed his wool sack, and dragged him to the side of the wagon. It took all of the brute's strength, but he wrestled Erik up the wagon gate and pushed him over the edge. Erik landed on his knees and forehead on the stony ground. His world went black.

The next thing Erik knew, he was under the wagon and trussed-up so that he was immobile. His head and knees hurt worse than the rest of his aching body.

"Gerna, are you all right?" Erik called out.

The rain was slamming down so hard on the wagon bed, it was hard to hear his weakened voice.

"A little worse for the wear, but I am better than these toadies are going to be when we get through with them!" Her voice was weaker than his.

"Don't get your hopes up, girly. Asgeir's clients can be pretty rough men," Haldor threw in.

"Asgeir, bah! She is here with us right now. I say we show her how rough we can be." Grimhald stared hard at Haldor in the fading light.

"No more talk of using her. She is a commodity, like a ring of cheese. We will sell her, and then we can get whatever we wish. So just shut up!"

"Seems like we should all get a vote," Konur offered.

"No! And that's final," Haldor stated.

The driving rain continued to fall.

———

HEIDI WAS beside herself as she huddled against Tor in the monsoon. They were cuddled tightly under Tor's oil cloth, their only protection from the storm. They knew they were still somewhat above the Nordra River and had no idea where their children were. This storm would surely wash away any sign of the horses and wagon passing. When the storm ended, they would work their way downslope until they made the river, then follow it until they found tracks. The storm would make it impossible for the criminals to move without leaving tracks in the soft ground along the river.

But, for now, they were stuck on the plain in a storm that should not happen in the middle of summer. Heidi took in as much warmth as she could from Tor and shared all she had. She knew the darkness would last about six hours. Sleep seemed out of the question, but somehow, when she opened her eyes, the rain had stopped, and the sky held the first hints of a new day coming. But, when she moved, every muscle hurt. Every joint was stiff with no desire to move. She quickly learned that Tor felt the same way.

When she pulled off the oilcloth and struggled to her feet, there was not enough light to see anything in detail. She and Tor used the time to stretch tired, stiff muscles and sore, painful joints. As they became aware of their surroundings, they noticed the horses had not wandered far away.

Mustering the strength and wind to whistle or call them was another matter.

The horses were contentedly grazing less than a half league distance. Walking toward the animals and talking about their plans loudly finally got the attention of the horses. Soon, they were mounted on wet saddles with empty stomachs. Another miserable day had started.

CHAPTER 13
NO SIGN

When Tor and Heidi made it to the river, it was flowing bank-full and very fast.

"We won't be crossing that this morning," Tor said.

"Let's work along this side. Surely the storm stopped them, too. We should at least find their camp," Heidi added.

"Keep to the brush line. Maybe we can surprise them," Tor said.

They worked along the edge of the brush, keeping a screen of vegetation between them and the upstream river channel. After about a league, they found some horse tracks in the mud near the river channel. The horses were moving upstream as Tor had expected.

Then they came to a gravelly area with bigger stones, and the horse tracks disappeared. It was now nearly two hours after sunup. They continued searching further upstream.

After an hour on that hard packed surface, they still had found no tracks.

"I cannot believe this," Tor said.

"I know, there must be something here on this side of the river." Heidi sounded frustrated. Hunger and exhaustion added to her melancholy.

"Have you seen any edible plants? We need some nourishment if we are to keep going," Tor said.

Heidi looked around, and her eyes were drawn to the slope out of the river valley. There was some color on some shrubs along the upland slope. She pointed. "Are those berries I see on those bushes?"

"Food!" he said.

"I will feel guilty eating while my children are missing." Heidi looked down and shook her head.

"We will be of no use to them if we are too weak to fight when we find them," Tor said.

"I know, but..."

"Mm, crowberries!" Tor exclaimed.

"We are saved. We can eat and pick some to take with us. In the lower parts of the plants, the rain did not damage them like on top. There are plenty for the picking," Heidi replied.

Soon they were back on the search with full bellies, and Tor's oil cloth tunic stuffed with the sweet fruit.

"I wonder if we passed them. Could they have crossed the river farther west, and we missed them?" Tor asked.

"I don't know. It sure seems we should have found something by now. But those horse tracks were moving this way," Heidi observed. "Let's go this way until we can cross the river."

They continued upstream weaving from the riverbank to the edge of the floodplain, scouring for any sign. They found nothing before midday. They ate some more berries, allowed the horses to rest, graze, and drink their fill of water from the river, then they made one more loop on the north side of the river, moving upstream. Tor went to the riverbank while Heidi worked to the upland on the north side.

Heidi made her turn back toward the river and was crossing a hard gravel area when something did not look quite right. Just to her side the gravel had been ever so slightly altered. She got off the horse and looked closer. There for less than a pace was a wheel track in the stones. It appeared to be moving east.

"Tor! Over here! Come Quick!" Heidi yelled at the top of her lungs. In a couple minutes, she heard his horse coming at a gallop. She flagged him to stop before he made it to her location. He dismounted and came to her. She showed him what she had found.

Tor picked her up and swung her around. "We must have been following them all morning. This gravel is so hard, the tracks don't show up! You are amazing. I wonder how many times I have seen something like that and missed what it was."

"It is a slim piece of evidence, but at least it is something," she said.

"Let's see what else we can find." Tor had his spirit renewed.

Another hundred paces farther on, a small creek passed through the hard gravel band on its way to the river. There was water running in the creek. They could easily see where the wagon had crossed the creek and was moving east.

"You can see when the five horses followed the

wagon. Our two bigger horses are still pulling the wagon," Heidi observed from her saddle.

"Yes, the only discouraging part is the water that splashed when the wagon got back on the hard gravel is already dry. We are at least an hour behind them," Tor added.

"And it's already midafternoon. Maybe we can move faster now." Heidi looked as far east as she could see. There was no movement beyond waving grass and bushes in the wind.

The trail became easier to follow as the river got smaller. There was less gravel and more vegetation as they neared the river's headwaters.

"Look, two horses split off and go toward the river," Heidi said.

"Searching for a place to cross, I suppose. But the wagon is still following the band of gravel to the east," Tor replied.

"Wait, those horses are coming back. They stopped here, to talk, I expect...and here the wagon turned toward the river. Let's go!"

Tor and Heidi followed the wagon to the river. The river was not even knee deep to the horses at that place. They crossed it easily and noted the wagon did, too. Then it continued southeast.

"Going for the Hvita River now, I think. If I

remember correctly, someone told me there is a cart track that links Borg to the trail from Reykjavik to Goddalir and on to Glaumbeer. There is a port there. Perhaps the villains are planning to sell our children into the slave market. Egill says there is slave market there despite it being illegal in Iceland. That might explain why our children were taken. Still, we better stay on their trail. If their destination is somewhere else, we might lose valuable time if we don't follow them."

"My ears hear your words, and they make sense, but my heart tells me we have wasted too much time looking at empty tracks," Heidi replied.

————————

GERNA'S BODY simply shut down when she was dragged under the wagon. She did not feel her abductors remove the wool sack she had been in since they were taken. She had no knowledge of the way the men groped her breasts while they were tying her arms and wrists, then her ankles and knees. She could not feel how roughly they handled her.

Erik could only look on while his sister was being manhandled under the wagon as the rain continued to pound down all around them. Tears trickled down his cheeks as he endured his own pain from being bound in the hot wool sack and bounced around on the bed of the wagon for most of the day. Now his elbows were tied together behind his back, his wrists lashed together, his knees and ankles tied tightly together, and a rope connecting his hands and ankles. He was painfully immobilized. *Where are Mother and Father? Please God, give us hope.*

Gerna woke up to the sounds of men snoring. There was no light, but the rain had stopped. She looked around while her eyes adjusted to the darkness. Gradually, she was able to see that everyone was sleeping except her. She could move her head, but even that shot pain through her bruised body. *Must endure. Mother and Father are coming.* She tried moving her hands. They were tightly bound at her wrists. She could wiggle her fingers, but even that hurt.

Gerna felt body heat on both sides of her. As consciousness slowly entered her mind, her sense of smell kicked in. The bodies pressed against her were two of her captors. The dirty scent of male sweat told her it was not Erik who was close. She would not be able to get away from these men without waking them. Once again, she was engulfed in depression.

I must think! If I lay here feeling sorry for myself, I will fail when I need to act. I need a plan. But think as hard as she might, she could see no way of escaping these outlaws.

She heard a stirring, then a cough. A shadow sat up. It leaned out from under the wagon. The man got up and left the protection of the wagon. The one pressed against her back stirred. He reached around and squeezed her breast.

"Ready to feel a man, pretty miss?" a voice hissed in her ear. He pressed his hardened manhood into her hands tied behind her back.

She reacted by grabbing the exposed organ as hard as her bound wrists wound allow. Then she threw her head back as hard as she could. Her skull connected violently with his nose, breaking it. The minor victory gave her strength, and she twisted his softening manhood painfully in her hands.

"Ack! You bitch!" he yelled out and tried to get away from her. But her grip on his penis was like iron. He reeled as she twisted relentlessly.

Now everyone was awake. Haldor came back and demanded what was happening.

"Your little puppy here decided he would try

his luck with me and found it was not a good idea."

Gerna strained to reply, keeping her twisting grip on Konur's manhood.

"Get this bitch away from me!" Konur cried out.

Grimhald crawled over and grabbed Gerna's forearm. "Let go, lass, he's finished hurting you," he said to her in a calm, reassuring voice. She let go, and Grimhald unceremoniously dragged Konur out from under the wagon.

"That bitch is a wild animal. I am going to teach her some manners!" Konur exclaimed. His nose was bleeding profusely as he was trying to put himself back together. His penis was almost too sore to touch as he tucked it back into his trousers.

"You will do no such thing," Haldor said. "In fact, you won't touch her again."

"Hah, you are not always guarding her, I'll get my chance," Konur said smugly.

Suddenly, steel flashed in the dim starlight. Konur was surprised to feel Haldor's axe breaking through his upper ribs and deep into his chest. He died with an astonished look on his face.

"That goes for all of you! None are to molest

the girl. She is our ticket to the future, not a plaything on this trip. Am I understood?"

"She's just a Skræling," Halvar said.

A fist to his jaw knocked Halvar on his back. Grimhald stood over him.

"What did you say?"

Halvar touched his chin. His jaw hurt like it was broken. He remained silent.

"Anyone else care to question my authority or decisions?" Haldor asked the rest. "Somebody throw Konur's body in the river. Pack up, we're getting out of here."

"But it won't be light enough to see for at least two hours," Ingvar protested.

"Shut up and move!" Grimhald commanded.

When Gerna was pulled out from under the wagon, she said, "I need to take care of my personal business."

Haldor replied, "Fine. I will untie your feet and knees. You don't need hands for that. But my axe is right here, in case you have something stupid in mind."

The northern lights were still waving green and lavender lights across the sky when they started. That gave Haldor enough light to navigate up the river valley.

"This hard gravel will allow us to move faster, and it does not even leave a track in most places," Haldor told Grimhald. "You lead the horses on another trail. Try to stay on the stony surface. We need to move away from here quickly."

"I will lead the others. I don't believe those two need those wool sacks today." Grimhald indicated the two prisoners on the bed of the wagon.

The party moved toward the east as fast as they could. Haldor could see well enough to maneuver the wagon along the gravel band that paralleled the river. He was surprised when they only encountered one small creek crossing their path. When they started to rise toward the headwaters, the gravel band became narrower, and the horses fell in behind the wagon.

Just before midday, Haldor sent Grimhald to the river to find a crossing. He was only gone a short time, came back, and reported he found a good ford very close. They crossed the river and followed a low valley to the southeast. When they reached the Hvita River, they would find a little used cart track that would take them east to the Nordra River.

CHAPTER 14
MEAT

The horses struggled to pull the wagon to the top of the ridge between the Nordra and Hvita Rivers. They were staggering when they finally reached the crest. Looking back and not seeing pursuers, Haldor ordered a stop to rest the horses. The sturdy animals grazed and drank a little water from the water skins they had filled before leaving the river behind.

While they rested, Erik and Gerna were allowed to take care of their personal business while being carefully watched. Both had shoulders and arms that were numb and useless anyway. They would not have been able to fight. Gerna thought about her small knife hidden in her dress but knew it would be futile to go for it.

Halvar scouted down toward the Hvita River a short way. Just down slope he saw a valley coming in from the north. On the slope was a boy about ten years old tending a flock of sheep.

"What are you doing up here all alone?" Halvar asked the boy.

"Our farm is just over there." He pointed southwest on the north slope of the Hvita River. A low ridge blocked the view of the small farm.

"I want two of your sheep. We will pay you for them when we come back this way in two weeks," Halvar said.

"I must ask my father before I can sell them," the boy replied.

"What is your name, boy?"

"Finn Annarsson, son of Annar Sveinsson," the boy announced.

Good, never heard of him—he won't know any of us.

"Well, come, I will take you to my leader. He will decide what your sheep are worth," Halvar said.

"My father will decide that," Finn answered.

"Of course. Bring your sheep."

In a few minutes, the sheep were moving into

Haldor's view. He saw Halvar and a boy following the sheep. *What is this?*

"I have found us some meat," Halvar announced to Haldor.

"I don't recall sending you for meat. What are you talking about?"

"Just over that hill, I found this boy tending to these sheep and thought some fresh meat would help on our journey."

"That is a good idea. We will take two. Boy, sort out two of your meatiest, and we will take them," Haldor told Finn.

"But I must go find Father and get his say so, if I am to sell any sheep."

"We don't have time for that. Sort out two fat sheep and be gone."

"I cannot do that."

"You can, and you will. Tell your father some foxes got two of your sheep. Now, sort them out or my men will."

"But..."

Haldor approached Finn, drawing his axe from his belt.

With tears flowing down his cheeks, Finn sorted out two good sized animals.

"Now, be gone with you, and if anyone follows us, they will die!" Haldor told the youth.

"What is your name, son?" Erik piped up, sounding compassionate.

"Shut up, you!" Haldor shouted.

"Finn Annarsson," Finn replied.

Haldor swatted him across the face with an open hand. Blood trickled from Finn's mouth.

"Your sheep will be replaced," Erik replied, scowling at Haldor.

Haldor walked over to Erik and punched him in the gut. Erik absorbed the blow and winked at Finn. Finn smiled, turned, and herded his sheep back to where Halvar found him.

"All right, let us get moving. Halvar, kill and gut those sheep. Then you can ride on the wagon while you strip the meat off the bones. Gerna, you can start planning how you intend to cook that meat next time we stop," said Haldor.

The day did not get as hot as the previous couple days had been. There were enough clouds in the atmosphere to block the sun. Also, the glacier Langjokull was in view and cooling the air somewhat.

As they descended the slope toward the Hvita River, the cart track became visible in places. It was not used much, and grasses covered most of it. But its imprint was visible from quite some distance. The shadows were getting long by the time they reached it. Haldor just crossed the cart track and went on to a small copse of scrubby trees by the river.

When Haldor turned the wagon around, he started ordering people to set up camp. A small creek entered the river just upstream. They let the horses drink and staked them out to graze in lush grass.

"In a few days, there will be no more lush grasses for the horses. We should cut some and store it on the wagon while it is plentiful. Ingvar, you tend to that. Halvar, you collect whatever firewood you can find. Grimhald, you help me get the prisoners taken care of. Those trees look strong enough to hold a man, don't you think?"

"They will suffice," Grimhald agreed. He untied Erik's feet and guided him over to the largest birch tree, which had a trunk diameter almost as thick as a hand width. He ordered Erik to sit so he could secure him to the tree.

"Wait, I need to relieve myself first," Erik replied.

"Hurry." Grimhald untied Erik's hands and

elbows but brandished his axe to show Erik he could not get away with any escape attempt.

"Well, Gerna, do you have great plans for how you are going to cook the meat?" Haldor asked as he began untying her feet.

"Since all we have is some raw sheep, no fat, no spices, no pans, I guess we will have sheep on a stick. What we don't eat tonight will be cooked, so it should last a few days. But why do you trust me to cook your food?" she asked.

"There is nowhere you can go. And you know that in order to survive, you depend on me. You take care not to rile me, you live another day. That simple," Haldor answered confidently.

"Yes, that answers my question." *What a fool!*

———

TOR AND HEIDI kept to the shadows and coves as they ascended the hill up from the Nordra River. The tracks indicated the outlaws were headed over the ridge to the Hvita River. They had to be careful not to be seen from the ridge. There were plenty of places ahead for an ambush. They hoped to overtake them by dark or shortly after.

"There is something we need to consider, my wife," Tor said as they rode along a shadowy draw.

"Which is?"

"We have not had any solid food for a couple days. We do not know what those men brought with them. We are getting light-headed from eating only cowberries. Can we fight in this condition?"

"You had to remind me how hungry I am. The answer is 'yes.' I can fight for my children after my navel meets my backbone. I was not even thinking about food. Now, you got me wanting to eat a grown moose!"

"Sorry."

"Let's just find them and worry about ourselves later."

"My heart hears you, my wife, but my stomach does not."

"You are welcome to go home and eat, if you must."

"You are right, let's go find them."

They made it to the end of the little draw. Looking up toward the ridge, Heidi saw movement. "Is that them?" she whispered.

Tor looked close but could not identify what he was looking at.

"Sheep," Heidi said positively. "Maybe the shepherd will let us buy one," she mused.

"Let's get up there and talk to him," Tor said.

"I hope it is not a trap."

"And there is that."

They worked their way up the hill. When they got close, the boy tending the sheep tried to hide, but Tor caught up to him. "Do not be afraid, I will not harm you," Tor assured the youngster.

"I do not worry for me, it is my sheep I worry about," the boy answered. "Earlier today some men came and took two of my sheep."

"Some men?" Heidi asked.

"Yes, they were mostly mean. But one was tied up. He said my sheep would be replaced."

"Did you hear his name?"

"No, the meanest one told him to shut up when he asked my name. His voice was friendly. When I said my name, the mean one slapped me and told me to leave. Then he told me that anyone who follows them will die."

"What is your name?" Heidi asked.

"Finn Annarsson, son of Annar Sviensson."

"Pleased to meet you, Finn. You will get some sheep back. How long ago did this happen," Heidi asked.

"It was just before midday. They have made it to the river by now," said Finn.

"Can I offer to buy another sheep from you, Finn?" Tor asked.

"I don't know. They are my father's sheep. I brought them out for fresh grass today. Our farm is less than an hour walk from here. We could go ask Father," Finn replied honestly.

"Perhaps on our way home, Finn. Those bad men took our son and daughter. They were the ones tied up. We need to get them. If we can, we will stop on our way back home." Heidi replied.

"Why did they take your children?" Finn asked.

"They are mean men. How many did you see?" Tor asked.

"There were four, plus the two tied up."

"Are you sure there were not five. We have been following five horses plus the wagon."

"I'm sure I saw five men, including the one who was tied up. But one of the horses looked like it had dried blood on its side. Maybe one got hurt," Finn offered.

"Could be. We must get going, the sun will be down before we get to the river as it is," Tor said.

As they worked their way down into the valley, the shadows grew. They were in cool shade most of the time, but they were running out of daylight rapidly. They were still an hour from the river when the sun dropped behind the ridge between the two rivers. They were cast into dark shadow, making it difficult to see the trail. Tor noted the driver was making tight switchbacks moving down the long slope to keep from losing control. Smart man.

As darkness descended on them, Heidi thought she caught the flicker of a campfire in the dark vegetation close to the river. *We are close!*

When they were still out of hearing range, they stopped and dismounted. The only weapons they had were their belt knives, so they had to get very close.

As they moved toward the river, Tor noted that his wife could still move like a ghost. She moved silently as a breeze.

———————

GERNA PREPARED a fire ring with a good view of the slope coming down to the river.

"Not there, you fool! Make that fire behind the thick brush. We don't need any sheep farmers coming into our camp. Now, do it right, or I'll tie you up again and not give you any food," Haldor scolded Gerna.

She got the fire going and had strips of mutton cooking soon. She felt much better just being able to move around uninhibited. She was still sore, but freedom of movement canceled that somewhat.

She is definitely trying to signal someone behind us. I think it would be very unwise to stay here. The horses have had a drink and little rest. We need to put some space between us and whoever might be coming down that hill.

"All right everyone, eat in the saddle. We are leaving this place, right now! Get in the saddle as quickly and quietly as you can," Haldor ordered.

"I thought we were going to get some sleep," Ingvar groused.

"Just do as I say and be quiet about it."

"Only a third of the meat is cooked and the fire is too hot to put out quickly," Gerna pointed out to Haldor.

"Leave it. The meat will spoil before we get another chance to stop, and who cares about the fire," Haldor replied.

Gerna quickly put the rest of the meat on sticks around the fire and added more firewood to keep it going longer. She hoped her parents were not far behind. She also thought they might appreciate some cooked meat.

They started up the cart track to the east. In the moonlight, Haldor could see some old wheel tracks.

"Grimhald, Halvar, and Ingvar ride your horses right behind the wagon to obscure the wheel tracks," Haldor ordered.

"Who do you think is after us?" Halvar asked.

"Not sure anyone is, but we don't want any company until we get these two sold," Haldor lied. He assumed Gerna was trying to signal her parents.

After two hours of rushing along the cart track, Gerna said, loud enough for all to hear, "Erik, I think Mother and Father's horses can move faster than this wagon. When do you think they will catch us?" She was good at planting doubt in Haldor's mind.

"Shut up," Haldor hissed.

She is right. I need to get this wagon off this cart track. They will follow the horses in the dark because it is easier.

"Grimhald, come up here," Haldor called back to his closest friend.

"What is it?" Grimhald asked when he rode up next to Haldor.

"We are going to split up. Tell Halvar and Ingvar to follow the cart track with the four horses. You and I will take the wagon up a creek to the north and hide. Our pursuers will follow the horse tracks, but they won't catch them because the wagon won't be slowing them down. When daylight comes, have them pick an ambush spot. I believe only two horses are following us. Tell them to shoot the woman, but don't kill her. The man will stop to take care of her. Put the second arrow in him when he tends to her. Is that clear?"

"Good plan," Grimhald replied before he eased back to tell the others.

Soon they came to a shallow creek. Haldor and Grimhald turned up the creek in the gravel channel. Halvar and Ingvar understood their orders and continued on, obscuring any tracks coming out of the creek bed on the cart track.

CHAPTER 15
TOO LATE AGAIN

Tor and Heidi crept toward the silent camp. *Hard to believe they have no guard posted.* Heidi contemplated what that meant. She could smell meat still cooking over dying coals behind some thick shrubs.

Tor came up to her from the side, shaking his head.

"They have left!" he exclaimed.

"What? When?"

"Over an hour past, I would say. The horses were watered in this creek, and they grazed a short time on the lush grasses. The people ate some meat, judging by the discarded skewers over there where the wagon was parked. I have a feeling they know we are after them, or at least they think we are. They left in a rush because there was a lot of meat still cooking on sticks around the fire."

"That was Gerna's doing," Heidi said, but did know where the words came from.

"How could you know that?" he asked.

"I know. We better get back to the horses and get after them. If they can follow that cart track in the dark, we can follow their trail."

"We are taking some of that cooked meat to eat along the way. If Gerna left it for us, I am sure going to eat it!"

It took them half an hour to get back to the horses and nearly that long to pick a trail through the bushes and brush to get back to the abandoned camp. Once on the cart track, they were able to move along at a ground-eating trot. Seven horses moving up that trail marked a path that as easy to follow.

———

HALDOR FOLLOWED the creek bed for several paces until he found a place where he could ease out of it, leaving little evidence. He continued along next to the creek until it curved behind a hill between it and the cart track. They would get some sleep and wait the whole next day, if necessary, for their pursuers to pass. Either Haldor or Grimhald would watch their back trail all the way to the cart track from the top of the hill by their campsite.

Grimhald was assigned watch while Haldor settled in for some much-needed sleep. About an hour before the sky would begin to lighten for a new day, he snuggled up behind Gerna. Erik and Haldor were snoring loudly.

"Are you ready for a man, yet?" Grimald whispered in Gerna's ear.

She was awake because she had heard him coming down the hill.

"Grimhald!" she said in mock surprise. "What would Haldor say?"

"I care not. You are too beautiful to waste on slavers. I want you first. We can always tell them Konur raped you, so we killed him."

"You have it all planned out. I like that," she whispered. "How about you untie me, and we can go past those shrubs for a little privacy?"

"You are giving up so easily?" he asked skeptically.

"I've been watching. You are the best man here. So strong and decisive. No wonder the men fear you."

"Do you fear me?"

"A little, but I respect you. You will be a great warrior." She laid it on thick.

"All right, but do not do anything stupid."

"Oh, I won't," she cooed.

They silently walked about fifty paces, then she led him into a small clearing. "Let me get this dress off, then I will lay on it," she said. As she took the dress off, she slipped her hidden knife blade into her hand. Next, she laid down on her dress onto her side. She worked hard not to grimace when the movement aggravated her sore muscles and bruises.

He started to get on top of her. He had removed his tunic, trousers, boots, and socks.

Gerna nearly gagged at his offensive odor. "Wait. I want you to lie on your side, like me. I want to feel your manhood. I want to know what is taking me."

"That is a strange request from a virgin."

"Don't you want me to be different...to be special?"

"You are different for sure. Just don't do what you did to Konur."

She chuckled and reached for his waist.

Suddenly, excruciating pain struck his privates and inner thigh.

Expertly, she slid the knuckle-long blade across the base of his rigid penis, through the skin of his scrotum, and into his inner thigh as fast and deep as she could. Hot blood gushed all over her hand, belly, and crotch. She quickly pushed back, rolled away from him, and ran up the creek. She then crept into some brush to hide.

Grimhald screamed in agony. "You bitch! You killed me! Haldor, help me!"

Haldor ran to Grimhald as quickly as he could find him in the dark. The moonlight had faded behind some clouds, and it took Haldor several minutes to reach his friend. By that time, Grinhald was weak from loss of blood. His crotch and upper leg were on fire. His pain was worse than any he could imagine.

"What happened here?" Haldor asked. At first, he did not see all the blood due to the darkness. When he noted that Grimhald was naked, which infuriated him, it took all his control not to kick his suffering friend.

"I told you not to touch her. What have you done, you fool!?" Haldor screamed at Grimhald.

"She...she. It's getting dark, Haldor. Don't let

me die. Help me! I...can't...f-feel..." Grimhald dropped his outstretched hand and closed his eyes for the last time. He said no more.

Gerna creeped through the bushes back to the camp. She quickly sliced through Erik's bindings and whispered for him to be quiet. "We must get out of here, fast. I will take Grimhald's horse and ride bareback. You get the wagon going. We must leave!"

"W-where is your dress?" Erik asked hurriedly. "And you're all bloody."

"Long story. Let's get out of here, now!" she replied.

The wagon horses were not hitched. Erik grabbed each lead rope and jumped on the back of Inga, the mare. Gerna jumped on Grimhald's gelding, and they made for the cart track.

Haldor kneeled and had his hand on his friend's forehead. He could tell he was still alive but did not know for how long. In the wan light, Haldor could see how pale Grimhald's body was. He was contemplating what, if anything he could do for his friend. In the dark, he was not even sure of the nature or extent of Grimhald's injuries. He was still trying to think of what could have happened when he heard the sound of the three horses galloping away from the campsite.

Haldor jumped up and ran toward the creek, axe in hand. When he got past the screening bushes Grimhald and Gerna had been hiding behind, he could only hear the horses splashing down the creek toward the cart track.

"Ahhhh!" Haldor shouted. "All for nothing! I will make them all pay for this!"

CHAPTER 16

FOUND

"They are killing two our best horses, moving so fast! Those horses need much more rest than they are getting. It will be hard to restrain me when we catch them," Tor said.

"You know I care for the horses, too, my husband, but my children fill my every thought. By the time Erik and Gerna are safe, there may not be anyone left alive to punish," Heidi replied.

They continued up the cart track as fast as they dared push their horses. It was close to an hour later when they heard horses coming toward them from the east.

"We need to get off this cart track and hide, quickly. Somehow they have discovered us coming and plan to stop us. We have no idea what kinds of weapons they are wielding!" Tor called to Heidi as he slowed and turned into the heavier brush on the south side of the cart track. She followed him. They got behind a birch thicket that barely screened them from the cart track.

The sky was just beginning to show the first gray of a new dawn when the running horses drew near. Heidi positioned her horse so she could see the track and drew her belt knife—the only weapon she had in her possession. Tor did the same.

Out of the dim gray came a shocking sight. Erik was fully dressed and riding Inga, the white mare, bareback while holding a lead rope to Kari, the white gelding. They were moving at a fast run. Then came Gerna astride a strange gray horse. She was naked, and her lower torso was covered with drying blood.

Heidi gasped, "Gerna is badly wounded. Has she been ravished and escaped?" She moved her horse out onto the cart track. The elation and relief on the faces of both children caused their mother to break down in tears. She nearly fell off her horse.

"Mother!" Gerna gushed. "I cannot tell you how glad I am to see you!"

"I am equally happy to see you, but what happened to your clothes?"

"Long story, but since you are here, we have more pressing issues to resolve. There are three more outlaws that need to be dealt with, and we need to get the wagon."

"How did you escape?" Tor asked, trying not to look at his naked and bloody daughter.

"Yes, that is a story I am eager to hear, too," Erik proclaimed.

"It will take too long to tell. We need to get back there before Haldor gets away!" Gerna asserted.

"Wait. What weapons do these outlaws have? As you can see, we did not bring any. What are we up against?" Tor asked.

"Haldor has an axe, but he is not a threat against four of us. Halvar and Ingvar are farther up the cart track and are sitting in ambush. Each has an axe, and they have one bow between them," Gerna said. She was anxious to get going.

"Where are your dress and shoes?" Heidi asked.

"Close to our camp site. We need to catch Haldor before he gets away," Gerna emphasized.

"All right, but where did all that blood come from?" Tor asked, as he started a slow walk up the cart track.

"Grimhald thought he was going to have me for a plaything until I surprised him with the knife Mother sewed into my dress. Thank you for that and for teaching where to cut a man."

"God, do I want to hear more?" Tor asked, looking up at the dawning sky.

"Both you and Mother have always taught us, 'You do what you must to survive.' That is exactly what Gerna did. I am proud of her." Erik's smile went from ear to ear as he glanced at his naked sister.

"Well, let's go finish this up so we can get back home. Hopefully your dress can be saved. We certainly do not have another," Heidi added, shaking her head in disbelief.

"It's a bit bloody, but hopefully I can wash it in the creek."

"Did you take it off because it was bloody?" Tor asked.

"No, I was lying on it when I spilled Grimhald's blood."

"I don't think I want to know any more." Tor cringed.

"I do. I want every detail. But first tell us about this Haldor," Heidi said.

"Haldor was the same bully who stopped us on the way back from the market five years past," Erik said.

"Yes, then he came up with this big scheme to sell us to a slave trader somewhere in the north. The same group. A little older, but no smarter, it seems," Gerna added.

"So that's why he took you east from our farm and was taking you to Glaumbeer," said Tor.

"That's the place. He said there is a market for Skræling half-breeds," Erik contributed.

"How much farther up this cart track?" Heidi asked.

"The creek is just coming into view. The camp site is a short distance north, behind a hill. No telling where Haldor is by now. Grimhald was supposedly his best friend. Gerna cut him pretty badly. Who knows how long he may have lingered. Haldor seems like he is fairly smart, but he is also unpredictable. Last night, he untied Gerna and had her cook that sheep meat." Erik was trying to think what else to say about Haldor when he saw a black spot far up the cart track.

"There he is!" Gerna exclaimed as she pointed up the trail.

"Erik and I will go get him. You and your mother go see if you can find your dress and get it cleaned," said Tor.

Gerna and Heidi turned up the creek. *No telling what we will find at that campsite,* Gerna thought. They followed the wagon tracks. It had not moved. The wool sacks the outlaws used to capture them were laying on the wagon bed. Gerna dismounted and found out how sore her feet were from all of the activities the night before without wearing her shoes, which were on the wagon bed with her woolen socks. She put those on before going another step.

With Heidi right behind her, Gerna walked around the stand of brush she had coaxed Grimhald around. The dead man's clothes were gone, and a pile of rocks apparently served as his grave. At least Haldor did that much for him. Her dress was nowhere to be found either. A more careful inspection indicated that Haldor must have covered Grimhald with the dress before piling the rocks on it.

"So, this is where it happened?" Heidi asked.

Gerna nodded, looking at the ground.

"If I was to guess, I would say that you seduced that young man to come over here where you could bend him to your will. His guard was down because you made him think you were going to give yourself to him." Heidi looked Gerna in the eye and saw the truth. "Very smart, child. Where did you ever get that idea?" Heidi asked.

"It was not hard, Mother. All the way from that overlook by our farm, I was forced to hear what this one or that one was going to do to me. Fooling those imbeciles with the promise of sex with a virgin was too easy."

"I assume you still are a virgin. I mean, this Grimhald did not get the reward he was seeking before you did what you had to do. Right?"

"Of course, Mother. It was ugly enough just getting close enough to smell him."

Heidi looked into the clear, blue sky and quietly whispered, "Thank you."

"Shall we make you a dress from that beautiful wadmal while we wait for the boys to get back here?" Heidi asked.

"I think we should hurry and go help them track down the other two culprits."

"Yes, good idea. I almost want to kill one of the good-for-nothings, myself."

"First I want to wash myself and the material in the creek. It was quite smelly last time I had it on!"

They shared a laugh. Heidi joined Gerna in the creek where they washed each other thoroughly with water and fine gravel.

"You poor dear, you are bruised from head to toe," said Heidi.

"Since I saw you on that cart track, I have not felt a thing." Gerna's eyes filled with tears as she threw her naked body against her mother's. They hugged and cried for several moments.

"Times like this remind you of how special the special people in your life are." Heidi sobbed as she led Gerna out of the water.

Using Heidi's belt knife and the binding twine the outlaws used to keep their prisoners bound, they fabricated a passable pants/dress for Gerna of the plain brown wadmal sack she had lived in for two days. Gerna insisted on the pants part because she planned to ride Grimhald's horse all the way home.

As Tor and Erik approached Haldor, he looked

back. He pulled his axe and Grimhald's from his belt and held them out to each side.

"There is nothing else you can take from me! You killed my best friend, you killed my future, you probably killed my chances of getting back to Borg alive. What else do you want from me?" Haldor asked, looking at Tor, not Erik.

"I took nothing from you. Anything you have lost is your own doing. Do not blame your actions on others. It makes you look small and stupid," Tor answered.

"You brought that Skræling whore back from who-knows-where, and honest, pure Norsemen are paying the price. You have destroyed a good man in Ferrminn Homallarsson, and now your half-breed son has taken all my future from me. You are all worthless scum!"

Haldor cocked back his arm and threw his axe at Tor. Tor easily ducked, and the axe flew past and landed on the cart track. The axe had not landed yet when Haldor charged at Tor, drawing his other axe back. Tor jerked his horse around and sped away just before Haldor arrived. Erik turned his horse away avoiding Haldor's fury.

His momentum caused Haldor to trip and fall on his face in the cart track. The defeated man rose to his knees and cried. "This can't be happening to me!"

"You captured my children and tried to sell them into slavery. What should I do with you, Haldor?" Tor shouted from beyond axe-throwing range.

"Give your farm to a real Norseman and go back to Vinland! No real Norseman wants you here!" Haldor ranted.

"My family and I get along fine with most people. What have I done to you?"

Haldor turned to continue walking up the cart track. He had only gone a few steps when three more horses could be heard approaching from the west. He pivoted to see Heidi and Gerna riding up with Grimhald's saddled horse on a lead. Gerna was wearing a cut up version of the sack she had been captured in. She was riding bareback on a white horse.

Haldor looked at Gerna and shouted, "Now what? Do you want to slice my scrotum up, too? Why didn't you gut Grimhald while you were at it? You're a half-breed Skræling whore! And probably a cannibal, too! I didn't look. Did you eat his testicles or just look at them? What kind of animal does that to a man?"

"What kind of man thinks he can take innocent people and sell them into slavery? What kind of man thinks he can rape a woman at his will? What kind of man thinks he is better than another? What kind of man are you, Haldor? Grimhald came into camp while you were sleeping, thinking he could just take me like I owed it to him. What kind of man is that?" Gerna asked.

Haldor cocked his right arm back and charged at Gerna from over fifty paces away. He just kept coming. Tor, Erik, and Gerna turned their horses and trotted out of the way. Heidi stayed put, pulled out her belt knife, and casually threw it. The blade buried to the hilt in Haldor's chest. He looked down, disbelieving. He dropped to his knees, then to his belly. A pool of dark red blood began to form under his body. Heidi rode over, dismounted, rolled Haldor over with her foot, reached down, and pulled the knife from the corpse at her feet. She wiped her blade on his tunic, turned, and remounted.

CHAPTER 17

TWO MORE

Heidi looked at her children, who looked back at her with open mouths. "Did you say there are two more like him up the trail?"

"Yes, Mother, let's go get the rest!" Gerna nudged her horse forward.

Tor and Erik caught up, but no one talked for a spell.

"Erik and Gerna said these other two are supposed to have an ambush set up, so caution is the word. Keep a watchful eye for any place that might made a good ambush location," Tor warned.

"You mean like that rock up there with the arrow pointed our direction?" Heidi asked.

"How can you see that from this distance?" he asked.

"How many times have I heard you say that my husband? I just can. You already know that."

"I know, but it always amazes me."

"I can see it. Can you, Erik?" Gerna asked.

"What side of the rock is it on?" Erik asked.

"Well, how should we handle this?" Tor asked Heidi.

"They wanted Gerna, so how about we just send her in to talk to the warrior. Maybe she can get him to take his pants off."

"Mother!"

"Just kidding, dear. We have two axes, and we are pretty sure they have two axes and that bow. In about fifty to sixty more paces, we will be in range for a long shot. It sure would be nice to know where the other man is."

"I will go around that rock, out of bow range to the north, and move around to the south to see if I can spot the other," Gerna offered.

"You have put yourself in enough danger for one day, sister. I will go." Erik started his wide circle around the rock protruding from the north side of the cart track. There were other rocks close by, but that one was by far the largest. They were close to the headwaters of the Hvita River, and the trail was climbing rapidly.

"I believe I will take a look to the south," Heidi said. She started her loop, leaving Tor and Gerna to stare at the arrow pointing their direction.

"I have not seen that arrow move since we got here," said Gerna.

"That's better than me. I cannot see it at all," Tor replied.

"I am beginning to wonder if it is a decoy. Perhaps to make us think someone is there, but really they are set up farther ahead. Maybe Mother and Erik are playing right into their hands."

"A dangerous thing to check out."

Gerna nudged her horse toward the rock.

"Don't, Gerna. It could be a trap!"

A running horse could be heard coming from the east, nearing the rock. Erik burst past the rock and stopped when he saw Gerna coming toward him.

"It's Mother! Her horse was hit and went down. She is trying to find cover, but there is little to be found where she is," Erik called out to Gerna.

Tor rushed to find out what was happening. Erik repeated what he had told Gerna.

"Where did the arrow come from?"

"There is a ditch between here and the river. The bowman is in that ditch and the other one is there too. They are about a bowshot apart. Mother is lying flat on the ground behind her horse. The bowman cannot get a good look at her, but he has protection so he can get closer. I don't have a weapon I can use here," Erik proclaimed. Then he showed Tor where the two people were.

"All right. Erik, you ride a loop between the ditch and the river. Be sure to stay out of bow range. Gerna, you ride in behind your mother. If you can get to her, load her on your horse and bring her back here. I will go down that ditch and confront the other outlaw. Your job, Erik, is to distract the bowman so Gerna can get your mother out of there. Let's go!"

Erik started his dangerous loop. He would need to make the bowman think he was in range, but not really be in range. Gerna would need to hope Erik distracted the bowman long enough for her to get her mother out before they were noticed.

Tor left his horse north of the cart track, out of range for the bowman, who was trying to get closer to Heidi. Tor yelled out a Lenape war cried to get everyone's attention. When the second man saw how close Tor was, he turned to confront him.

Tor advanced on the man like he was leading a hoard of Norse raiders into an unarmed monastery. His cold blue eyes promised death and destruction.

Ingvar thought he could keep Halvar with an open view of the plain from the cart track to the river. He became confused when a rider circled from the north. Halvar was set, waiting for the rider to come into range. Then Ingvar saw the woman circling in from the south. Halvar immediately changed targets, shot, and fatally wounded the woman's horse. When she went down, Ingvar saw the sun flash on the blade of her axe. So, now Halvar was working himself along the shallow ditch to get close to the woman, who was hiding behind her dead horse.

Time was limited by the late hour. Perhaps an hour of decent light was left. After that, Halvar's bow would be useless.

Ingvar waited for the determined man coming toward him. He had no time to see what was happening to Halvar. He was momentarily distracted when the one on the horse rode past him toward the river. *Where is he going?*

Halvar was afraid to get up and look at the woman. He did not see a bow when her horse went down, but he couldn't be positive. *Better safe than sorry.* He knew it was not Gerna. But suddenly, there were three people working toward him and Ingvar. The rider coming around from the south was becoming worrisome. *If he gets much closer, I will be exposed.* In his panic, he launched an arrow. It landed well short of the rider, but at least he stopped. But then, he started coming closer again. Halvar shot another arrow at the rider. It also landed well short of the mark.

Thinking about the rider, Halvar did not register the sound of a galloping horse behind him. As he watched, the rider turned and went back to the east. Looking that way, Halvar noticed a man with an axe walking toward Ingvar. *How did he get there?* About then, Halvar noticed the galloping horse behind him. He spun around to see the two women on a galloping horse, moving west. He snapped off a quick shot, but it missed wide to the left. Then, the horse was out of range.

Halvar turned back to see the man bring his axe down on Ingvar's shoulder. Blood cascaded into the air as the axe sank deep into Ingvar's shoulder. He fell backward, and the man went down on top. They were out of sight, but Halvar saw the axe rise and fall again. He assumed Ingvar was gone. He thought Haldor and Grimhald would be along any minute now.

For now, Halvar was the only one of his friends left alive on this battlefield. He thought about that. *I have seen Erik and Gerna riding horses on this battlefield. Had they escaped or been rescued? With Ingvar gone, I am truly all alone. I have six arrows left, but it will be dark long before I can use them. I am outnumbered, and my situation is hopeless. Without my friends, I have nothing to go back to. Die fighting? That might get me to Valhalla, but I doubt it. I have not really fought with valor.*

Maybe I could trade our four horses for my life. Then what?

Out of a nightmare, Tor Eriksson stood in front of him. Tor was brandishing a bloody axe. *Ingvar's blood.* Then came a woman's voice.

"That one is mine!"

It is the Skræling, Tor Eriksson's wife. She may eat my heart!

"I surrender to Tor Eriksson." Halvar looked at Tor with pleading eyes. "Please don't give me to the Skræling. She may do something unnatural with my soul."

"It was too late for my mercy when you killed my horse, not to mention taking my children and running our good wagon horses too hard too long. I won't even mention the way you mistreated my children and made my husband and me miss several days chasing you. So, what is a fair punishment for all you have done?"

"I-it was all Haldor. He made all this happen. The rest of us went along because he promised us wealth," Halvar pleaded.

"Still, you tried to kill me...and killed my beloved horse instead. I don't recall Haldor being here to tell you to do that," Heidi replied.

Gerna and Erik joined the group.

"Halvar, here, claims that Haldor coerced his friends to act as they did. What do you two say about that?" Heidi asked her children.

"He seemed to take as much pleasure in hurting us as any of the others, and he was all in favor of having their fun with my sister," Erik replied.

"He said it was not important if they hurt us because we were just Skræling half-breeds," Gerna added. The look in Heidi's eyes of motherly protection for her offspring made Halvar cringe.

"It is late. What should we do with him?" said Tor.

"We could put him in that other wadmal sack

and make him ride back to our farm bouncing on the wagon," Erik suggested.

"Fair enough. For now, since darkness has fallen on the land, let's go camp on the river. Maybe we can catch a fish or two for a meal, then get some sleep. The next few days will be long and hard," Tor declared.

Tor made Halvar use his axe to open an area in the ditch to bury Ingvar. Halvar thanked the gods for darkness, so he did not get a good look at Ingvar's horrid wounds. Once buried, he gathered enough rocks to cover the grave to keep the foxes from digging it up.

At the river, they bound their prisoner to a small willow tree. Erik and Tor set about finding enough dried branches for a fire while Heidi and Gerna used their hands to attract a couple fish. After a few misses, they managed to fling a couple nice trout up onto the bank.

All of them slept until the sun broke over the eastern mountains and woke them up. The sun reflecting off the Langjokull glacier was so bright, it hurt their eyes.

After another meal of trout, they gathered the eight horses and moved back to Haldor's camp site. On the way, they found that foxes had found

Haldor's body and scattered the remains far and wide.

The other wadmal sack was still on the wagon. While Tor and Erik got Kari and Inga hitched to the wagon, Heidi and Gerna placed the foul smelling wadmal sack over Halvar's head, securing it to his body with ropes around four places. Unlike Erik and Gerna, Halvar's wrists were bound in front, making his condition much more comfortable.

Tor, Heidi, and Gerna rode saddled horses while Erik drove the wagon. Tor and Erik would trade off driving the wagon back to their farm.

On the way, Halvar was a cooperative prisoner, offering no complaints. During the second day, they stayed on the cart track along the Hvita River. Riding behind the wagon, keeping an eye on Halvar, Gerna found herself feeling sorry for the man. His sweat was bleeding through the wadmal material in the hot sun. When Tor stopped the wagon to rest the horses at the campsite where Gerna had cooked mutton on sticks, Gerna's empathy was strong.

"I think we should take Halvar out of that hot sack," Gerna stated.

Everyone looked at her with blank stares.

"It is inhuman to confine a person in one of those sacks."

"You spent two full days in one. Now you want to free one of the men who did that to you?" Tor asked.

"Not free him. Just take the sack off. We can keep him bound and still let him breathe fresh air."

"If you say so, sister." Erik climbed onto the wagon and began untying the ropes confining Halvar to the sack.

"Do I get a say in this?" Heidi asked.

"We should vote. In favor of taking the sack from the prisoner, raise your hand." Gerna looked at the others with her hand raised high. Erik raised his hand next. Tor looked at Heidi, shrugged his shoulders, and slowly raised his hand. Heidi looked at her husband's and her children's faces and saw peace in their eyes.

"Make it unanimous." Heidi raised her hand and smiled at Gerna. *She has become a wise woman, no longer a child.* She could not be prouder of her daughter.

"Thank you, Erik. I don't know how much longer I would have lived with that hot sack covering me."

"Thank my sister, it was her idea to get that off you."

"Thank all of you. You are treating me better than I deserve. If there is anything I can do to repay the harm I have caused, I will gladly do it."

"You do owe me a horse. And not one of those poor beasts you and your friends were riding. I don't know how you will pay for it, though. I doubt you have seen enough treasure to cover it in your whole life." Heidi sneered.

"I would work for you day and night, if you would allow me the privilege," Halvar pleaded.

"Wait. Two days past you were trying to kill us. Now, you want to be a thrall on our farm. Your behavior does not match your words. What game are you playing now?" Tor asked.

"No game, my lord. I was led down the wrong path. I should have known better, been a better man. I could see no other way and followed the wrong leader. But all of you have shown me honesty and integrity. I am willing to subject myself to thrall status until I prove myself worthy of those labels." Halvar sounded sincere.

"We could let him stay in the barn and work off his debt. If he is as worthy as he claims, he can earn his freedom and move on. If he proves as worthless as he has shown up until now, we can take him before the Thing court and have him outcast for three years," Gerna suggested.

"Very mature of you, daughter. What are your thoughts, Erik?" Heidi looked at her son and husband with no expression.

"In church and Bible study, they talk about forgiveness and giving second chances. He killed an expensive horse. It would take a long time to work that off. If he is willing, I guess he deserves a chance," Erik said.

"I think I would rather talk about all this without Halvar listening to every word. But, if the rest of you are willing, we may be able to work something out. We need to let Egill and Cairenn weigh in on it, too. Their safety could be affected, as well. And I need to go see Gothi Garmr to make the legal arrangements," said Tor.

"I would like to go with you, Father," Erik added.

"Me too," said Gerna.

It took them two more days to take the cart track along the river to Borg and on to their farm. Halvar was a model prisoner the whole way. They ate fish that Heidi and Gerna managed to catch and cook on willow sticks over small fires.

Before they passed any farms, they stopped to bathe and wash their sweat-soaked garments. Erik, Tor, and Halvar had thin wool summer tunics, trousers, woolen socks, and leather boots. Halvar's boots were worn and scuffed beyond repair, but they were all he had,

Heidi wore a linen riding dress featuring a split skirt. It was getting well-worn and tattered. Gerna only had the wadmal sack that they had improvised into a sort of coverall outfit. Her boots were still serviceable, but she had worn holes in her woolen socks. None of them had a hat, or any type of head covering.

After scrubbing their bodies with sand and thoroughly rinsing, along with washing the dust and sweat from their clothing, they all felt better. Although, as a group, they still looked ragged and worn.

CHAPTER 18
HOME

Cairenn and her daughter, Heidi, were the first to greet them at the farm. Both had long red-orange hair that flowed generously over their shoulders and down their backs. Green linen dresses with high buttoned necks and short sleeves dropped from high waists to cover their bare feet. They appeared to be twins, but the crow's feet around Cairenn's smiling eyes betrayed her thirty years.

"Glory be, look what the cat dragged in! We was about to give ye up for dead." Cairenn ran to Heidi and gave her a big bear hug the second she dismounted. "Aye, and ye smell plenty ripe, too," she said when they separated.

Cairenn then looked at Gerna. "Holy Mother of Mary, what happened to your clothes, girl?"

Cairenn's Heidi, fourteen years old, looked at Halvar with a thousand questions in her eyes.

Egill and his son, six-year-old Egor, stepped out of the hall and joined in the welcoming. Tor proceeded with introductions and suggested the returning party get cleaned up, put fresh garments on, and meet in the hall for a great meal. Egill and Egor volunteered to tend to the horses and wagon.

"You can come with me, Halvar. I will lend you some clothes and show you around a bit," Tor said to the transfixed man still in the wagon.

Halvar was still in shock that he was no longer bound like a prisoner. Then, when he laid eyes on the girl with the long, wavy red-orange hair, green eyes, and body displaying the blooming of a beautiful maiden, he was completely disoriented. And her looking back at him with curiosity in her eyes —he was gobsmacked.

Cairenn, her Heidi, Erna, Gerdis, and Unndis went to work putting a large pot of beef and vegetable stew together. The heretofore lost family members looked famished. They were all anxious to hear how they came about having a stranger in their midst.

When they were all gathered at the table, the stories began. Erik and Gerna described their ordeal from their abduction to their rescue. Tor told of his and Heidi's pursuit and frustrations until they watched Erik and Gerna galloping out of the morning mist. They were shocked to see Gerna naked and riding bareback on a strange horse. The three younger Torsdottirs looked at their older sister in awe as Heidi described her belly covered with blood and handling the charging steed with only a lead rope and her knees.

The stories continued until nearly dark when Egill pointed out there were two cows and four goats that needed milking in the barn. Not to mention setting up Halvar suitable sleeping quarters.

The gathering broke up with promises of more stories the next day. Young Heidi looked on longingly as Tor, Egill, and Halvar left the hall for the barn.

Her questioning eyes did not go unnoticed by her mother or the older Heidi.

"What be on your mind, me child?" Cairenn asked pointedly.

"Just curious how an outlaw becomes a part of the family." she replied.

"Now, darlin', 'tis your mother you're tryin' to fool, not your father. You had more than that in your googly eyes when you were watchin' that boy eatin' his stew. Mind ya, you're not marryin' age yet. And he'll be long gone before you are. So, don't go doing nothin' you're goin' to be regrettin'. You hear?" Cairenn was remembering her own actions, at the same age, when she met Egill.

"Oh, Mother, you embarrass me!" young Heidi replied.

"Well, just see to it that the two of ya don't end up alone in the barn or some other place. Agreed?"

"Yes, Mother," a red-faced Heidi answered.

The older Heidi had her back turned with a wide smile on her face. Promiscuity did not hold the negative perception in the land of her youth that it did among Christians. It was difficult to understand. Yet, she was relieved that Gerna was still a virgin after her ordeal. *Being forced is different than giving oneself freely*, she rationalized.

"There's something I am trying to understand, Tor," Egill said when he and Tor walked from the barn to the hall.

"Which is?"

"You say this Halvar put an arrow into Heidi's prized horse, helped abduct Gerna, wanted to rape her, and planned to sell her into slavery. Yet, here you are, making a home for him, giving him clothes, and letting him work off his debt. I would have thought you would have just killed him and been done with it."

"Egill, you're the last person I would expect to question giving a man a second chance."

Egill stopped walking and remained quiet. *Yes, it was Tor who gave me a second chance after I dared touch his wife. I am an idiot!*

"You are right, of course. Sorry I asked. You have a way of knowing a man has a good side."

"Always ask. Just make sure you're asking the right question. It was my family who saw the good in Halvar before me. Gerna, the victim said it first. She is an amazing woman. A week past, she was a girl. Now she is a mature woman, a shieldmaiden, no less. Killing a man for the right reason when you are fourteen years old is no easy task for a man raised among warriors. I cannot imagine her mindset as a Christian girl. We need to keep an eye on her for a while. She must have many divergent thoughts about her actions and her future."

"Spoken like a great father."

Soon, everyone was settled into a routine on the farm. Erik, Gerna, young Heidi, and Egor would get to the barn first to milk the two cows and four goats. Some of the milk was for use in the house while most was used to make cheese. Tor, Egill, and Halvar would feed and water horses, oxen, cattle, and any sheep that were confined for various reasons, including lambing, breeding, or doctoring.

———

WITH TOR'S BLESSING, one day Erik and Gerna loaded up four sheep in the cage cart, pulled by Inga, and started for the farm of Annar Sveinsson. They would be gone four or five days. They followed the cart track to Borg and turned east on the track along the Hvita River.

By sheer coincidence, they met Finn and Annar bringing a wagon loaded with sheep for market a few hours east of Borg. It was late in the day and a good campsite was at hand, next to the river.

Finn was surprised to see Erik and Gerna free of the rough men. He was not sure if he should be friendly or not, since it was weeks after Erik promised he would get his sheep back.

"Hello, Finn. We are happy to see you again," said Erik.

"How did you get away from those men?" Finn asked.

"You should introduce us to your father first. Then we will tell you why we seek you out."

"All right. Father, this is Erik and Gerda. Erik said we would be paid for our sheep that they stole from me. Erik, this is my father, Annar Sveinsson."

"Glad to meet you, Annar Sveinsson. My sister is Gerna, not Gerda. I can promise those thieves will not return for more of your sheep."

"How can you promise that? Are they dead?"

"All but one, and he is now working for us. He was in the wrong place at the wrong time and ended up with those bad men. He is a different man now."

"The men of God say there is redemption in every man."

"This is a good place to camp. We have food and would be happy to share if you care to join us," Gerna offered.

Annar looked at Gerna questioningly before responding, "We could never impose. We need to be at the Borg market with these animals tomorrow. The earlier, the better."

"No imposition on our part. And an early start will get you there in plenty of time. These four ewes are the sheep my brother promised. We can go back to Borg with you, and you can put these in with your lot, or take them back to your flock—your choice."

"I thought you only took two sheep. Why four?"

"It was a traumatic experience for Finn. He showed great bravery against some very bad men. We wanted to reward him. These sheep are from the prized flocks of Tor Eriksson and are excellent breeders. You earned them in an unfortunate incident."

"I could not accept your generosity, Erik Torsson. One of your sheep is equal to two of mine."

"Your animals saved our lives, Annar. It is our privilege to be able to repay you. We insist." Gerna gave Annar a stern look that said the deal was final.

Erik and Gerna were able to return home two days early, to everyone's surprise. A new round of dinner table stories was in order.

———

WHEN THE LIVESTOCK was taken care of, everyone would meet in the hall for morning meal. Heidi,

Cairenn, Erna, Gerdis, and Unndis prepared the meal, set cups, plates, spoons, knives, and whatever else was needed on the table. Morning meal was usually barley or self-sown wheat gruel, smoked pork, cheese, and bread.

After everyone got their hunger sated, Gerna, young Heidi, Erna, Gerdis, and Unndis would clean the table and wash the dishes. When those chores were done, Heidi and Gerna would go to the barn and work with the horses.

The mother and daughter pair had a way with horses that amazed Tor. Heidi had never seen a horse until she got to Iceland. Instead of being timid around the big, powerful animals, she went right into their pens, talked to them, and made friends immediately. Soon, she had them doing whatever she wanted. Tor forbid Heidi from riding the horses until Gerna was born.

After she was born, Heidi brought Gerna to the barn every day. Gerna acquired Heidi's skills with the horses just by being around and following her mother. By the time Gerna was ten years old, she and Heidi were a team. They did things with the horses Tor and Egill only dreamed of. Tor was always amazed that Heidi could get a saddle on a horse before anyone else dared try.

"It's all in the telling them it is good to carry a human," she said. "The way is to convince the animals that we are their friends. Show them you will do anything for them, and they will do anything for you."

About midday, everyone would meet in the hall again, usually for some of Cairenn's soup or stew and stories about the morning work.

In the afternoon, Heidi and Gerna would take Erna, Gerdis, and Unndis riding out on the farm somewhere. Tor, Egill, Halvar, and Egor would ride out to check the various sheep flocks. Each had two dogs that guarded them, so worrying about the foxes getting to the sheep was not necessary. Keeping the dogs fed and active in the winter was another matter.

They would always take combs to harvest wool from some of the sheep. That was a continuous job, for the sheep would produce wool faster than they could harvest it. Sometimes it was necessary to get the women and children involved to keep the sheep from getting too shaggy and the wool from getting too matted to comb out. With the addition of Halvar to the workforce, tending the sheep became less time consuming.

After a month at home and everything running

smoothly, Tor announced it was time to go meet with Gothi Garmr Hallrsson to establish Halvar's status. The next day, Tor, Heidi, Erik, Gerna, and Halvar saddled their horses and started for Hallr-landstedr.

Garmr introduced his grandson, Bjorn Valborgsson.

"Bjorn has seen seventeen winters and is now a judge on the Thornes Court. After the Althing next summer, he will be the gothi in my place. I am sixty-two now, and it is time for me to step back. Bjorn has been studying the law since he could walk, so I think he is qualified," Garmr explained.

"Glad to meet you, Bjorn," Tor and Heidi said simultaneously, as both reached a hand out to shake Bjorn's. Tor quickly introduced his party to Garmr and Bjorn.

Gerna's black eyes locked with Bjorn's blue ones. *He is a handsome one. I wish I were two years older. I would like to get to know him better.*

Noting the interaction between Bjorn and Gerna, Garmr said, "Ahem, what brings you to my hall this late summer day?"

About that time, a blonde beauty wearing a dark-blue linen dress with white filigree on the front and around the collar walked into the room with cups and a pitcher of crowberry juice.

"Allow me to introduce my granddaughter, Asfrid Valborgsdottir. She is Bjorn's twin sister. She will be our guest until the Yule celebration in Reykjavik, where my son has a hall."

"Glad to meet you, Asfrid," Tor and Heidi repeated the scene from their introduction to Bjorn. Asfrid's beauty tongue-tied Erik, and he only nodded.

Why did Grandfather not tell me he had such a handsome guest when he told me to bring in the juice? She looked only at Erik.

Tor made the other introductions. Asfrid reached a hand out to each, but when she and Erik touched hands, they obviously held their touch for an extended period.

I always thought such beauty only existed in stories. Yule will be here too soon.

"Thank you, dear. You may return to help the maid clean up now."

"Actually, we were finished. Allow me to serve this juice, and I would like to listen. You know I am interested in the law, and these people may have a most fascinating case." Asfrid replied, shocking her grandfather. *She has never shown a minute's attention to the law. She only likes to ride horses.*

"As you like." He looked at her with questioning eyes. Her eyes had already turned to Tor's son.

"So, what brings you here today, Tor?" Garmr asked, noting that Erik and Asfrid were staring at one another, Bjorn was looking at Gerna with an odd smile, Gerna was looking into Bjorn's eyes with the same smile, Heidi was looking from one of her children to the other with many questions in her own black eyes, and the stranger, Halvar, was looking lost.

"We are here on the matter of Halvar here. He was caught up in some criminal activity in which he played a minor, unwilling part. The activity has been cleared, and now I would like to take Halvar in as a freeman worker on my farm. Halvar has incurred a debt with me, and I wish to house him on my farm until the debt is paid. He has nowhere else to go. When the debt is paid, he will be free to go where he pleases and work for whoever will pay him what he desires."

"What is the nature of this debt, and how long do you expect it will take Halvar to pay it?"

"The debt is the price of a horse that Halvar's

actions caused to die. It was a very valuable horse, and I expect it will be paid within a year."

"I see. Are there other details that should be brought up at this time?"

Halvar was dumbstruck when Tor referred to him as a freeman.

"Bjorn, do you have any questions for Tor?" Garmr asked.

"Uh, it sounds pretty straightforward." He looked away from Gerna with guilt in his eyes.

"Father, I think you should tell the gothi the whole story from the beginning. It would clear any questions and make your request more solid," said Gerna.

Everyone looked at her with astonishment.

"I like Gerna. She speaks from the heart!" Asfrid announced.

I did not think my daughter was even listening to anything but her heart beating for Bjorn. She has been amazing me and her father a lot, lately.

On Gerna's suggestion, Tor told of the abduction from start to finish. When he finished, he looked to Gerna and Erik for approval.

"Father, you should emphasize Halvar's repentance and willingness to work hard to prove himself. He does every job on the farm without complaint. Who do you know that does that? Surely not me!" Erik added.

Asfrid beamed.

"Erik is right, Halvar has worked very hard to please us." Tor looked to Heidi for support.

"Everything Tor and the children have said is true. Halvar found himself in a bad situation. He could not have stopped it either. The outlaw, Haldor, was bent on destroying us because of where I come from. I don't know how to stop such hate, but I am thankful for the strength of my husband and my children for fighting for themselves. And I am thankful for Halvar being the kind of man who admits his mistakes and is not afraid to take responsibility for his actions."

Halvar looked at Heidi with awe and humility in his eyes. Gerna looked to gauge Bjorn's reaction, he returned her look with profound respect. Erik looked to Asfrid, she looked back with admiration. Tor looked at Heidi with tear-filled eyes.

"Tor, I have told you before, you have an amazing family. I hope my grandson brings me good news from your clan as long as I live. Since Halvar is a freeman, and you have made your agreement for repayment of the horse, I can see no need for further legal action. The scoundrels have been dealt with, no person on your side has had sustaining injuries, all the loose ends seem to be tied up. Halvar, good luck with your future, wherever it takes you.

"Gerna, you have the kind of insight that would be put to good use on the gothar or at least in the courts. I hope you consider it. Women are unusual in such positions, but there are a few.

"Now, you people have a long ride ahead of you, and the days are getting shorter. Go with God."

Erik stepped toward Asfrid. She stood up and said, "Allow me to walk you to your horse." His smile hurt his cheeks.

"Yule will be here before we know. I would like to see you before you go."

"I desire that as well. We will find a way."

Suddenly, Gothi Garmr was at her back.

"Erik Torsson, I give you permission to call on Asfrid. Just make sure you bring some of your stories with you," Garmr said to Erik, who was shaking like a leaf.

"Tor, I think Bjorn would like a word with you."

"Yes, Tor Eriksson. If I may, I request that I escort you back to your farm and to call on Gerna in the future. When she gets a little older, that is." Bjorn talked faster than he could think.

"How about I send Gerna with Erik when he calls on Asfrid. That way you won't be out half the night, and the Gothi need not worry about you. And my daughter has proven herself to be capable of making mature decisions. You may consider her old enough to court."

"Thank you, Tor Eriksson!" Bjorn turned to Gerna, who stood next to her horse. "Did you hear that?"

"Yes. You may kiss me." She looked at Tor with smiling eyes. "Father, please turn and kiss Mother." She turned back to Bjorn and leaned into him.

Erik said to Asfrid, "As long as everyone is kissing." He pulled her into him. She pressed into him, their lips met and stayed pressed together several heartbeats.

"The road is long," Heidi announced, breaking up the promising couples.

They were an hour into the three-hour ride when Heidi said to Tor, "That was a surprise."

"What?" he teased.

"I think our family will be growing soon, by three."

"Three?"

"Yes, I think we are soon to have a gothi in the family. And it won't take Erik and Asfrid long to make it two. Then, Halvar and young Heidi will be right behind them."

"What? Halvar and Heidi? Are you sure? I did not know they even noticed each other."

"Remember, you didn't know it when Traveler and Corn Stalk got together either! You are blind to love. I am glad you actually saw me."

"I could never miss you, my love."

"Good answer! You are learning."

"You are my teacher."

CHAPTER 19

CHOICES

By mid-October, snow appeared in the highlands and temperatures fell below freezing most nights. The sheep's wool was growing fast, so extra hours were needed to keep their coats from getting matted. The sheep were gathered from the far pastures and the dogs employed to keep them close. All the children were old enough now to help with the combing, washing, and spinning the wool.

Heidi, Cairenn, Gerna, and young Heidi were busy daylight to dusk, and even through the long evening hours weaving wool fibers into various cloth materials. Some of those would be used to make clothes and other items needed on the farm. The surplus would be taken to the market in Borg where it would compete with cloth from other farms in the region.

The courtships between Bjorn and Gerna, Erik and Asfrid, and Halvar and young Heidi somehow found a way to blossom into full-fledged love affairs.

Word had gotten to Asfrid and Bjorn's parents that their son and daughter had found love interests north of Borg. Gothi Garmr arranged a lunch party at his hall for the parents to meet each other.

The day came, and Tor, Heidi, Erik, and Gerna loaded the wagon and set out on a cold morning for Garmr's hall. They would need to hurry to make it home before sunset.

It was a gray morning with a promise of snow in the air. The horses acted as if they enjoyed working on the cold day. As yet, no snow had fallen, but the track was frozen and old ruts made for a rough ride. Tor had to work to keep the anxious horses from running.

At last, their destination came into view. Garmr and his staff, with the help of Bjorn and Asfrid, had decorated their hall with willow and birch wreaths and twined rope strands. Those were covered with ground juniper boughs. It made for a festive, welcoming sight indeed.

No one had mentioned to their parents that Bjorn and Asfrid's love interests were Skræling half-breeds. It never seemed that it was important.

Tor gathered the presents he and Heidi had had made by local craftsmen. For Valborg Garmrsson, Tor had a set of ram's horn drinking cups made. The cups were made of horns from one of Tor's prized rams. They consisted of perfectly matched left and right horns and were decorated with silver piping. A silver Christian cross stood out in the center of each cup.

Heidi had a silversmith make a tea serving set made of polished silver engraved with filigree and tiny crosses. The set included four cups, saucers, stirring spoons, a tea pitcher, and a serving tray.

Tor knocked on the door, and a servant answered.

"Come in, Tor Eriksson, you are most welcome."

The four cold travelers entered the warm hall and smiled. The servant helped them remove their heavy wool overgarments and escorted them into the great room. The servant indicated their wagon and team would be cared for.

As Tor and his family entered the great room, Asfrid and Bjorn jumped up and rushed to their special guests. A quick peck on the cheek, and they turned to show off their love interests, holding hands in a show of solidarity.

Gersemi Valborgswife stood when Garmr did. She was dressed in a formal, dark-blue wool suit with gold thread trim. A large woman with a serious square face and cold, gray eyes, her blonde hair was tied in a severe bun on the back of her head and held in place with silver pins. She looked anything but friendly.

Valborg Garmrsson stood, entranced by Heidi's beauty. His woolen tunic was a rusty fall color, and his trousers were dark gray. He was big, like Bjorn, with a handsome face and warm, blue eyes.

Heidi wore a dark-blue woolen dress that was buttoned to the neck. White filigree decorated each shoulder, down over each breast, and along the button line from neck to slim waist. The skirt flared slightly, then followed her legs to the floor. Black leather shoes with white straps adorned her feet. Her waist-length black hair was braided and wound on her head and pinned in place with silver hairpins. Only a few gray hairs twisted through her braids. Her dark skin contrasted nicely with the white trim on her dress. Her black eyes were mesmerizing.

Tor had on a dark-green-colored tunic with black glass beads pinned in the high collar. Black woolen trousers covered his legs, and his black boots were highly polished. Around his waist he wore a black leather belt with a silver buckle featuring a horsehead engraved on the face.

Erik was dressed similar to Tor except his shirt was bright blue.

Gerna wore a green woolen dress with a high neck, buttoned to her throat. She had a silver chain belt on that gathered her dress to her slim waist. Her shoes had leather soles and green woolen tops that matched her dress. Her long dark-brown hair had a small braid from her forehead around tied with green yarn behind her head. Otherwise, her full hair hung to her waist, as was proper for a maiden her age.

When the introductions were finished, Gersemi gave Heidi a hard look.

"Are you from the Mediterranean, my dear?" Gersemi asked Heidi.

Taken aback, Heidi simply answered, "No."

"Well, your dark skin, I just wondered where you are from. You certainly do not look like an Icelander."

"No, I suppose not." Heidi tried to sound friendly.

"Then where do you hail from?" Gersemi, feeling the tension mounting, at least tried to sound friendly.

"I have mentioned Tor's fascinating story to Valborg several times over the years." Garmr tried to defuse the tension before it got out of hand.

"I am guilty of dismissing it as preposterous, Father. I never saw the need to trouble Gersemi with such a fantastic tale," Valborg confessed.

"Well, where are you from, dear?" Gersemi pressed.

"I was born in Long Pine Village, on the Spirit Water River. Tor and I became acquainted in Monongahela Village at the confluence of the Monongahela, Spirit Water, and Spirit Rivers." Heidi gave the woman an enigmatic answer.

"I am not familiar with those places. What country are they in?"

"They are in the Monongahela Nation."

"Never heard of it."

"It is not important, dear. The main thing is Heidi is here, and her son and daughter are the topic of our visit to Father's hall." Valborg tried to change the subject.

"I just want to understand where my possible future in-laws are from. It is important in some circles, you know." Gersemi stood her ground.

"Erik, do you enjoy working on a farm? My company deals with shipping. I could get you started in an exciting career on the sea, if you were interested." Valborg tried to change the subject.

"I am content producing quality livestock. Adventuring at sea and wars do not appeal to me," Erik answered honestly.

"And you, dear, what are your dreams?" Gersemi asked Gerna.

"I love our horses. I cannot imagine anything better than getting to work with the beautiful creatures every day. Although, I must admit that certain developments have recently piqued my interest in the law." Germa looked at Bjorn as she finished. He smiled his approval.

"I am done beating around the bush. I will not have my children associated with half-breed Skrælings. These children have no idea what they are getting into. There is no place in decent Iceland society for misfits. We will not tolerate our children associating with yours. You can take your family and leave this hall, Tor Eriksson!" Gersemi exclaimed.

Tor started to rise. Heidi's face turned red. Gerna and Erik looked at Gersemi in shock.

"Sit down, Tor," said Garmr.

"Gersemi, you are out of line! You do not come into my hall and demand that my guests leave. Tor and his family are fine people, and I will not have them mistreated under my roof. You will apologize, and we can start these discussions anew, or you can be the one to leave." Garmr was shaking, and his face was turning red.

"Now, everyone, please simmer down. We can work out these differences with a little patience and talk." Valborg tried to slow things down.

"Mother, I am bothered by your feelings. Where did that come from? You have always taught us grace and understanding. Now, put to test, you draw the first sword. What happened to 'We are all God's children and should treat others with kindness?' How many times did you say that when I was a child? Surely you do not stand by what just came out of your mouth." Asfrid spoke with a tear running down her cheek and Erik's hand tightly squeezed in between her hands.

Gersemi got up and walked unsteadily to the back of the hall. Valborg followed her.

"I apologize for my daughter-in-law's behavior. I am glad my wife, God rest her soul, was not here to witness that outburst," said Garmr.

"Perhaps we should leave and let things settle down here," Tor offered.

"Nonsense. I won't hear of it. She will learn to get along," Garmr said.

"Wife, that was a most embarrassing scene. What were you thinking?" Valborg asked Gersemi.

"It all seems unfair. Why should we be the ones to harbor those people? Why should we be the ones to live with 'others?' Why can't our children just find ordinary Norse mates instead of those...those horrible foreigners?" Gersemi implored, tears streaming down her face.

"To start with, my dear, no one is asking for any hands in marriage here today. We are just meeting people our children are attracted to. It is our job to get to know these people. They may be the greatest people in Iceland. They may be the worst. We do not know. That is why we are here— to get to know them. So, let's go back out there and see if we can determine what our children see in them. I have great faith in both of them to make good decisions. I thought you did, too."

"But she is so dark. Everywhere they go, people must wonder."

"Let them wonder! She's different looking. So, what? She is also beautiful...and so are her children. Leave it alone until we know them better. All right?"

"I will try." She wiped her eyes and nose again, touched up her makeup, stood, and straightened her clothes. "Please stand by me when I apologize." She grasped his arm and made him look at her. He nodded, and they returned to the great room.

"I-I wish t-to apologize for my behavior earlier. No one had told me to be prepared for this. I mean, I was just not expecting..."

"Apology accepted, Gersemi Valborgswife. I know I am different from anything you expected. You are a mother protecting her children. I understand. Now that the shock has passed, shall we see if we can bridge the chasm and get to know each other? I promise I am not a witch, nor are my children," Heidi said with a smile that reached her eyes.

"Those are wise words, Heidi Torswife," Gersemi responded.

"I think it is time we let my staff feed us the delicious meal they have prepared," Garmr announced, nodding to a woman wearing a full apron. Everyone took their places at the table just before plates of food began arriving from the kitchen.

The talk at the table bounced from childhood stories about the young adults at the table, to Tor and Heidi's adventures, to Valborg's shipping company, to raising sheep and harvesting wool, and everything in between.

Gersemi noted that her children were completely at ease with their chosen partners and seemed like they belonged together. She longed for the days before Asfrid was too young to think about marriage.

After the meal, Tor and Heidi presented the gifts they had brought for Valborg and Gersemi. A sincere thank you was expressed by each, along with another apology for rude behavior.

Tor said, "Perhaps we should get started on our way. I think snow will be arriving before we reach Rolfcarllandstedr as it is."

Erik turned, took Asfrid's hand, and addressed Valborg. "I know it may seem sudden, but I wish to ask your blessings for the marriage between your daughter and me. I know we are young, but I can promise I will always worship her and protect her from any evil."

"That is sudden, Erik Torsson. But the bond you two have formed is unmistakable. Still, I wish to talk this development over with my wife before I give you an answer. There are many things to consider. Please be prepared to answer some questions, such as what are your future plans? Where will you live? How will you provide for your children? Are you prepared to deal with the hate directed at you for your mixed-race marriage? One more thing. Asfrid's mother and I have begun negotiations for an arranged marriage for Asfrid. We will need to resolve that issue before I can answer you. But I appreciate you coming to me at this point. We will be here to take my daughter back to Reykjavik at the beginning of December. I will hope to have an answer by then."

"That is fair," Erik answered.

"I already have my answer, Father. Yes! With all my heart, I wish to be known as Asfrid Erikswife."

"Your mother and I will take that into account." Valborg looked to Gersemi who was dabbing her eyes with a handkerchief.

Tor and Heidi refrained from making any comment.

"We can wait," Gerna said so that only Bjorn could hear her.

Soon, Tor's family had mounted their wagon and drove off into a darkening gray sky. The first hour was snow free, and they discussed all the happenings at Garmr's hall.

"I would like to have heard what Valborg said to Gersemi after her little display," said Gerna.

"It does not matter. She felt threatened and spoke out. She apologized. No harm was done," Heidi added.

"Do you think they will bless your marriage to Asfrid, Erik?" Gerna asked.

"How should I know? She never said anything about any arranged marriage. I am not sure she even knew before Valborg mentioned it."

"Not a good note to end the day on, but I did enjoy talking with Valborg and Gersemi, after the early tensions were eased," Tor said.

Heidi kept to herself. She was thinking about where they would put Erik and Asfrid. They still had a couple empty rooms in the big hall, but she felt her family should have better accommodations than Egill and Cairenn. And if Heidi and Halvar should marry, where would they go? They would need another milk cow or two, and more milk goats. Many changes are coming. Yes, and the younger girls are no longer little girls. We will need another great hall!

They were still two hours from home when the first snowflakes came twisting out of a solid gray sky. There were just over two hours of daylight, but a storm could shorten that. As the horses plodded along, snow covered the frozen cart track first. Then, it began to stick in the grass. Soon enough, it was snowing harder, and the cart track was more difficult for Tor to see. Everyone stopped talking to help Tor keep track of the road.

In her mind, Heidi kept building her new hall. She even thought about Gerna's wedding. Should she add a couple of elements from her heritage? Would the Norse understand and tolerate that? So much to think about.

The snow was ankle deep on the horses when they turned onto their lane. Everyone was covered in a blanket of white and keeping their thoughts to themselves.

Heidi was back on Gerna's wedding. *Wouldn't it be nice to have Bright Star to discuss some of these things with? I wonder what she is dealing with. She was pregnant with her first child when we saw her last. How many does she have now?* Her mind drifted through swirling snowflakes in a gray background.

As she looked into the chaotic, jostling flakes with the dull gray background, a shape began to form. It was a tall hill covered with trees of every kind. The trees were in their autumn splendor with colors ranging from dull brown to gold to orange to red, with some evergreens mixed in. Her eyes followed down the hill until she saw gray smoke mixing with the colorful trees. Then a palisade came into view. She seemed to float through the overlapping maze-like entrance. Four large oval-shaped longhouses came into view. The smoke she saw in the trees was pouring from the long-house smoke holes. One of the lodges had a sentry post outside of it with a cattail head and leaf carved above head high. She brushed an elk skin aside and walked through the east-facing entrance. In the big room, several people were gathered. The first one she recognized was Water Mint. Her hair was plaited in one long braid. It was more gray than black. She wore a buckskin dress with long, fringed sleeves. Next to her stood Tallow. His hair was also gray and hanging in braids down his chest. He wore a buckskin shirt, breechclout, and leggings. Age showed on their once-

youthful faces. Six young adults stood around them, two were pregnant young women.

Past them was an opening to the head of the central firepit. On a low platform stood a white-haired Corn Stalk. She also wore a buckskin dress. Next to her stood a stoop-shouldered and white-haired Traveler. Corn Stalk made a gesture, and the crowd fell silent. "We are here to celebrate the changing of the Matron of New Long Pine Village. Today, Water Mint will hand her leadership to her beloved niece, Bright Star!" Cheers rang out from the crowd. Water Mint stepped forward and handed Corn Stalk a scepter carved in the shape of a cattail head and leaf. Corn Stalk turned and reached the scepter out to Bright Star. The new Matron of the Water Plant Clan and New Long Pine Village took the scepter and vowed to make every effort to rule as her beloved aunt Water Mint had these many years.

Something caught Bright Star's attention. She looked right at Heidi. "Sister!" Bright Star shouted, and ran right to her, wrapping her arms around Heidi in the strongest bear hug she ever experienced. Tears flowed from both their faces, and no words were exchanged. Many hands touched Heidi, and she felt a warmth she could not label. The scene began to fade.

Heidi heard, "Mother, please wake up." The

phrase was repeated several times before she realized they were talking to her. Her eyes flickered, and she heard Unndis shout, "Mother, you came back to us! We were scared!"

"I...I am all right, baby. I just had a strange dream. It was wonderful. But I missed you." She hugged her daughter like there was no tomorrow.

"I think you were lost in a vision. No one could wake you. You had a smile on your face, then you started crying. Gerna wanted to splash you with cold water, but I thought it best to let you finish. Where did you go?" Tor asked.

"You know me, husband. I was watching the snow, and suddenly I was descending into New Long Pine Village. Everyone was there. Water Mint stepped down as head matron and Bright Star was named the new Head Matron. Corn Stalk made the announcements. But everyone was much older—older than us! It was so real. All the children were grown and married. Where do you suppose that came from?"

"Sounds like you need a good rest. Come on, girls, we need to let your mother rest." Tor tried to shoo the twins and Unndis from Heidi's room.

"But she just woke up! We have not seen her all day," Unndis whined.

"Just go, let her be. And get yourself ready for bed. We will all talk tomorrow."

The storm let up by daybreak, leaving about two hands of snow on the ground. But warmer air from the south quickly reduced the snow cover to shady spots and ditches.

CHAPTER 20
WEDDINGS

CHAPTER 20
WEDDINGS

By November first, all the roads were open and dry. Erik and Gerna saddled their horses and headed for Hollrlandstedr. About halfway there, they met Bjorn and Asfrid.

"Just on our way to your grandfather's to see you two," Erik shouted as he brought his trotting horse to a halt.

Asfrid replied, "We wanted to come see you this fine day."

"Too bad we didn't pack a lunch." Gerna chuckled.

"We did." Bjorn laughed. They chose a spot and got off the cart track.

"Did you have any trouble getting home?" Asfrid asked.

"No, but just a bit before we got home, Mother seemed to slip into a kind of trance. It was like she was asleep, but no one could wake her. She finally woke up after Father got her into her own bed, but she went right back to sleep. The next day, she said it was the best dream she ever had. But she refuses to tell us about it. She says if she talks about it, the magic might be broken. Strange."

"Some dreams are very private," Asfrid said.

"Have your parents said anything about weddings?" Bjorn asked.

"I heard Mother and Cairenn talking something about needing a bigger hall or a new one. When they knew I was coming, they changed the subject. Why?" replied Gerna.

"Just curious, I guess. But I was thinking sooner might be better than later." He took Gerna's hand and said, "What do you think about a Yule wedding?"

"I'm thinking I won't be fifteen until midwinter. Maybe spring, or even Althing would be better. You will be gothi by the Solstice. That seems appropriate."

"Provided our parents agree."

"They will all be there, so it would be perfect. I will talk to Mother when we get home."

"We were thinking we could go to your home today and discuss it with them."

"Ooh, I like that idea. Let's eat and get going."

When Heidi saw four horses coming up the lane, she started to worry, then she recognized her horses and children. *Funny, I know my horses better than my children!*

"Welcome, children. You are traveling today!" Heidi greeted the young lovers.

"Is Father close by today?" Gerna asked.

A hammer sounding in the barn answered her question.

"We would like to have a discussion with you both," said Erik.

"I will go get some drinks made. You all go to the barn and get your horses taken care of and bring your father when you're done."

I wonder what revelations we are up against now. Heidi could not help wondering.

Heidi, Tor, Erik, Asfrid, Bjorn, and Gerna sat the table in the great hall. Each had a cup of plum tea, a piece of cheese, and a chunk of coarse bread. Young Heidi had Erna, Gerdis, and Unndis in the barn playing a hiding game.

"What is it you are anxious to discuss?" Tor asked.

"As you know, a month from today, our parents are coming to Garmr's hall. By the way, he wishes to invite you to come that day. He plans to detain our folks for a couple days to get this courting and wedding plans thing figured out.

"Asfrid and I have been discussing these things, too. We think we would like to arrange a double wedding, possibly at the end of Althing. I will be voted gothi by then and will need to reside in this district. Grandfather certainly has room for all of us in his hall. We wanted to get your feelings on the matter." Bjorn started the conversation.

They talked around different scenarios for a bit, but always ended up that Erik was needed on Tor's farm, and Gerna wanted to be there to work with Heidi and the horses. Complicating matters was the fact that Halvar and young Heidi were becoming more involved and would probably wed within a year. They would need a place as well, making Tor's hall more crowded.

"We should consider what your parents might be thinking," Heidi addressed Bjorn and Asfrid.

"At this point, I do not care what they are thinking, I want to spend the rest of my life with your son."

"Asfrid, you need to consider your parents

always. They have loved you your whole life and will never stop, no matter what you do. But having them on your side is a blessing."

"You left your parents and your whole country behind."

Heidi's eyes immediately filled with tears.

"Her parents were killed when she was eight years old."

"Oh, I am so sorry. Erik and I had not talked about that. I did not mean to be so insensitive."

"I know you were not being mean. You are forgiven, my soon-to-be new daughter."

"Wow, I had not thought of that part of it," said Gerna.

"Back to your parents, Asfrid. What if they want you to live in Reykjavik? Could you do that? Could you, Erik?"

"You know my place is right here on this farm, Mother. Asfrid's parents will need to understand that."

"We nearly had a problem with closed minds last time we met. You young people need to understand the world does not care about your whims. Sometimes you need to compromise and get along the best you can. Understand?

"Yes." Four voices chimed it.

"To sum things up, we agree to suggest a double wedding at the Althing. We will offer lodging here, but if Garmr insists, Bjorn and Gerna will move into his hall. If Valborg and Gersemi insist Eric and Asfrid live in Reykjavik, we will see if we can make some sort of a compromise. Is that it?" Heidi asked.

All agreed. The youngsters went to the barn to saddle Bjorn and Asfrid's horses. Some long kisses, and maybe a little more, took place before Bjorn and Asfrid started back to Garmr's hall.

December first arrived long before anyone was ready, but Tor's family was prepared to leave before the sun made its abbreviated appearance for the day. With only four hours of sunlight, they would not waste any time on the three-hour ride. Tor's family rode horses and brought two pack-horses with extra clothes and blankets. If discussions got out of hand, they may need to sleep in the cold barn.

At Garmr's house, they noted the decorations had been upgraded with some red ribbon accenting the green boughs on the hall. The effect was gayly festive.

In the hall, things were also warm. Valborg and Gersemi greeted Tor, Heidi, Erik, and Gerna warmly. Valborg brought several bottles of Madeira, and Garmr had an ample supply weak beer, strong beer, and mead.

Heidi and all four young adults stuck with the weak beer, Tor tried the Madeira but mostly drank strong beer or mead. Garmr liked his mead. Valborg and Gersemi had a glass of Madeira at all times.

Before the first drink was consumed, Asfrid asked, "Well, Mother, Father, am I betrothed to someone I have never met?"

Gersemi smiled and replied, "No dear. We had to pay a bride price, but you are free to marry Erik, if it still suits you."

"A bride price? For no bride? How does that work?" Asfrid wanted to know.

"The bride price was the first thing agreed to. It turned out that was the only thing the groom's parents cared about. The gothi we were working with suggested we just pay it to get out of the contract."

After a few afternoon drinks, dinner was served. A beef roast was the main dish, with side dishes before, during, and after. Finaly, a skyr was served to end the meal.

During the dinner, Bjorn expressed his desire

to have a double wedding at the end of the Althing the following June.

"Sure, why not? Everyone will be there already. It's a great idea." A slightly tipsy Gersemi agreed.

"Valborg?" Garmr asked.

"Yes, grand idea. It may be difficult to provide mead for the multitudes, but we'll figure that out by June."

"Now, about where we will live. Erik is needed on the farm. And I have no desire to live in Reykjavik my entire life. I have been to Tor and Heidi's farm, and I love it there!" Asfrid was feeling the beer, too.

"Bjorn, where do you and Gerna plan to make your home?"

"It is a little harder for us to decide, Mother. If I am elected to the Gothar, I will need to live in this district. But Gerna wants to continue working with the horses on the farm. True, we have a few horses here she could work with, but Grandfather has a limited amount of pasture for exercise and so on."

"You cannot count on this place, Bjorn. I am old and cannot maintain this big hall after I step down from the Gothar. I have already begun negotiating a sale," Garmr offered.

"I guess it is settled then. Our hall is filling up, husband." Heidi looked at Tor with a big smile.

"And you will need to keep all the grandchildren in food and clothes," Gersemi slurred.

"Bring them on," Heidi chirped.

Winter passed very slowly for both Erik and Gerna. Farm work was slowed by winter storms that brought heavy snow. Manure and used bedding had to be piled in the available spaces until fair weather melted enough space to load it on wagons and hauled out to fields and pastures. It was well past the spring equinox before the fields were open enough to spread the accumulated winter refuse.

Early spring lambs had to be kept warm for several days in the main hall, which meant constant cleaning, milking ewes, and bottle feeding the lambs. All the girls and Egill's son were anxious for spring.

It came and with it, mud. Every day meant washing smelly, muddy clothes in big wooden tubs. Cairenn, Heidi, and young Heidi spent their days in back-breaking labor washing and hanging wet clothing and bedding on rope strung in every available space to keep everyone in serviceable garments.

Tor, Egill, Halvar, Erik, and Egor worked sunup to sundown milking, feeding, and doctoring livestock. Erna, Gerdis, and Unndis spent their time milking ewes, bottle feeding lambs in a room in the hall, and cleaning that room.

Meals were unorganized and sporadic at best. Somehow, they all made it work. They lost only two of the more than twenty lambs, none of the four calves and none of the six horses born between March one and May one.

By mid-May, the hall was back to normal. Heidi and Gerna went to work on Gerna's wedding dress and Erik's formal clothing.

Halvar and Erik took over the task of taking wool and sheep to market, leaving Gerna to work with Heidi, Cairenn, and young Heidi on wedding plans and clothing for the entire extended family. The Althing was approaching much too fast. Cairenn and young Heidi volunteered to keep food on the table, giving Heidi and Gerna more time to work on wedding tasks. Tor, Egill, and Egor managed to get the farm chores completed every day. Everyone knew their responsibilities and tended to them.

"You said you were seventeen when you first laid eyes on Father, right?" Gerna asked Heidi.

"That was a lifetime and a world away. Why do you ask?"

"What was it like, seeing Father that first time?"

"It was wonderful and frightening. I had never looked at a man before. I mean, I had never been attracted to a man. Until that day, the only man I ever thought about was the war chief I had to kill. All of my thoughts I had ever had about men were how to cripple them. Where were the weaknesses? That sort of thing.

"Then there was your father. Big, strong, handsome. I was mesmerized." Heidi put down her sewing and looked past Gerna into the past.

"But you knew he was the one?"

Heidi blinked and shook her head slightly. "What? The one? Oh yes, I did not even know his name right then. I just knew I was looking at my future."

"How special. Bjorn was a surprise like that for me, too."

"I know. I was watching." Heidi took Gerna's hand and squeezed it. "I am so happy for you. Your young man seems to be a perfect match for you."

"He is, and he knows it, too. He feels the same

as me. We were meant to meet at his grandfather's hall that day."

The days featured more and more hours of daylight and warmer temperatures. Occasional storms blew through depositing needed rain, but never seemed to last long.

Finally, the day came when they pulled away from the farm with two heavily loaded wagons and six horses. In addition to the normal things they brought to Althing, they had their wedding clothes, and all the paraphernalia associated with the double wedding. When they set up their camp, there was an extra tent that was dedicated to wedding things.

Heidi spotted Valborg Garmrsson in the crowded tent city, and Tor was able to set up their camp right alongside. A few tense moments were had when Erik and Gerna spotted Bjorn and Asfrid standing aside, talking to very attractive young adults. Bjorn was seen joking with a pretty blonde girl in a well-made, form-fitting dress and bare feet. Asfrid was similarly occupied with a handsome young man with golden hair and trimmed beard. His tunic displayed powerful chest and shoulder muscles.

Erik and Gerna were the first off the wagon

and hurried to their betrothed partners. The issue was quickly resolved when Erik and Gerna learned the couple were first cousins on their mother's side and would be members of the wedding party.

The first week of the Althing was fairly routine with the usual law recitation and trials. A heated argument occurred at one of the trials. No agreement could be reached, and a blood duel was challenged. Each combatant wielded a sword and a shield. Each wore a chain mail tunic and a helmet.

The feud would take place in the center of the ring of judges, of which Bjorn was one. At the appointed time, the head judge gave the signal for the fight to start. Both warriors circled and feinted several attacks, but no contact was made for some time. The crowd was becoming restless, calling for blood.

Finally, one fighter swung his sword high. When his opponent raised his shield, the attacker swung his sword around low and struck his knee. The sword blade happened to strike the man right in the seam of the defender's knee guard. The blade slit through the leather joint and did severe damage to the man's knee. He went down, howling in pain.

The victor's sword was now wedged in the

down man's armor and knee joint. The man dropped his sword, reached into his tunic and pulled out a neck knife. He started for the head of the downed man, who was clutching his leg, screaming.

Bjorn noted the man moving in for the kill and yelled, "Stop! Enough! You won, Steinn. There is no need for further bloodshed on this field."

Everyone looked at Bjorn with a stunned expression. Gerna, who was there to watch "her" judge in action, started clapping. Soon others joined in. The slap of hands and chorus of "Mercy" thundered across the plain. The man with the knife tucked it back into his tunic and looked around shyly.

The head judge raised his arms to quiet the crowd. "Steinn Colmrsson, you have won the duel and the settlement. No charges will be advanced. Someone get this man some help. And clean up this mess. This court is dismissed!"

"Gerna, I believe you saved a man's life today," Bjorn stated when they all gathered for evening meal.

"I thought you did that when you told that Steinn to stop."

"I think the crowd wanted to see a death, but

you put an end to that. I think you have a good understanding of justice. You make an ideal partner for a judge and a gothi, Gerna," Gothi Garmr said. Everyone in camp clapped. "And Bjorn, your calling that execution to a stop went a long way toward your election to the Gothar tomorrow."

Heidi and Cairenn were all smiles as they handed out large bowls of beef stew, slices of cheese, and chunks of bread. Valborg, Gersemi, and Gersemi's sister handed out mugs of mead, beer, wine, and crowberry juice.

Throngs of onlookers gathered at the Law Rock when the Law Speaker, Thorkell Tjorvason, stood to announce the gothi departing the Gothar and their newly elected replacements. Garmr Hallrsson was hailed as the oldest and one of the longest serving gothi in Icelandic history. His replacement was the young Bjorn Valborgsson, grandson of Garmr Hallrsson. Four other gothi replacements were announced, but none received the applause accorded Bjorn.

The adults did not miss the fact that Erna, Gerdis, and Unndis had spent much of their free time at the Althing playing games and talking with three boys who appeared about their ages.

The three sisters competed in bow and arrow shooting and axe-throwing contests. Erna and Unndis won their age groups at the archers' range, and Gerdis defeated all comers, boys and girls, in the axe-throwing competition.

Three days following Bjorn's appointment to the Gothar, he was joined in a shortened Christian wedding to his beloved Gerna Torsdottir. In the same ceremony, Erik Torsson was joined with Asfrid Valborgsdottir. The couples rode away from the ceremony on white horses and one pack horse for each couple to a secret location to start their new lives together.

Many tears were shed by the families, but there was also some joking, laughing, and pranks carried out by certain younger members of the Eriksson household. Some of those pranks would be discovered when the newlyweds opened their bedrolls for their first sleep together.

"How long do you suppose the newlyweds will stay away from home?" Gerdis asked at the campfire at the end of the first day of travel back to Rolf-carllandstedr. When she looked at her sisters, a smirk was evident on her face.

"By tradition, they would lie around and drink

mead for thirty days. Some call it 'The Moon of Honey,'" said Tor.

"I think these girls have some secret they should share with us," Heidi said, after noting the suppressed giggles from her three youngest daughters.

"Then it wouldn't be a secret," Erna added.

"If it is such a big joke, we'd all like to get a laugh out of it," Heidi pressed.

Unndis was the first to break. "We put shredded grass in their bedrolls."

"Yes, wet shredded grass, and some bugs," Gerdis added, barely able to contain herself.

"Don't forget the horse balls. Hahaha!" Erna chimed in.

"You girls are incorrigible!" Heidi exclaimed.

"Aye, but I bet Erik and Gerna will be gettin' even. Then, we'll see who be laughin'," Cairenn offered.

"It'll be worth it." Unndis giggled.

On the last day of their return home, the sun was getting low as they made their way up the cart track. Heidi looked toward the lowering sun, haloed by high clouds that shimmered in gold and orange colors.

The shape of a mountain came into view. The

mountain was bathed in autumn beauty. Her gaze lowered as she admired the beautiful forest. Gray smoke feathered among the autumn leaves. A palisade came into view with four columns of blue/gray smoke rising above the palisade wall.

She found herself floating through the overlapping wall openings to enter the village. Children and nondescript dogs were running here and there, chasing, barking, laughing. All looked healthy and full of life.

Heidi drifted to the Water Plant Clan longhouse, pushed the elk hide door hanging aside, and entered. Her sister, Bright Star sat at the head of the central firepit. Her doeskin shirt was open, and a black-haired baby was suckling.

"Sister, you came back!" Bright Star exclaimed. "Are you well?"

"Yes, I am very well...and my heart sings to see you with your baby."

"He is Redbone, son of Red Hand, War Chief of New Long Pine Village."

"But my last visit you were so much older." Heidi was confused.

"Oh, that was a silly dream, I expect. As you can see, I am the same age as you. We will have a feast in your honor. How long can you stay?"

"I cannot stay at all. I must get back...my... children..."

Heidi jerked awake when the wagon stopped just outside their hall. "Home already? I must have fallen asleep."

"You have been having another of those 'vision dreams.' No one will pressure you for details." Tor looked at her with great concern on his face.

"It was a very pleasant dream, but very private. Thank you."

CHAPTER 21

CONCERN

The farm continued to prosper with new hands to complete all the tasks required of a sprawling sheep and horse farm. The men pitched in and soon had doubled the size of the main hall to accommodate the five families living in it, plus room for future growth as the remaining Torsdottirs matured to marrying age.

During the year following the weddings of Erik and Gerna, a much smaller wedding was celebrated at Tor's hall when Halvar and Hryn—she had decided being called "young Heidi" had gone on long enough and insisted people use her middle name—were joined. The ceremony took place at Rolfcarllandstedr and was mostly Christian but included a few pagan elements.

Also, that first year, Harald Eriksson and Inga Bjornsdottir came into the world. Both Harald and Inga seemed to take on Norse characteristics with the exception of Inga's hauntingly big, black eyes.

On the return from Althing, Heidi once again slipped into one of her "vision" dreams. This time she had to be carried into her bedroom and did not wake up for hours. She acted perfectly normal after she woke up and maintained her dreams were beautiful, but private. That did not stop Tor from worrying about her. He was perplexed how she could go into some sort of trancelike state and come out of it when she was ready and suffer no other consequences. She seemed to be completely comfortable and happy whenever a dream occurred, but she was completely oblivious to the world around her. *What if she slips into one of these dreams when she is alone with the babies? It could lead to disaster.*

Tor spoke to each of the family members privately about his concerns. While they had the same concerns, none knew what to do about it. "Back in Norway, me mum knew of a sorceress who might help, but that was long ago and far from here. I suggest one of us is always with her until we find someone who can help, master Tor," Cairenn said.

"That's the best we can do for now, I guess," Tor conceded.

Long periods of time elapsed between Heidi's dreams, but they always popped up when least expected, usually near the end of a long wagon ride. She still insisted they were happy dreams that belong only to her.

———

THE YEAR ERNA and Gerdis turned seventeen and Unndis turned fifteen, three more weddings took place at Rolfcarllandstedr. While Erna and Gerdis remained on the farm and their husbands integrated into the farm family, Unndis went with her husband to live in Reykjavik. His name was Brian Bagott, a second-generation Icelander from Dublin. He worked for Valborg Garmrsson at his shipping company. As the population of Iceland grew, the demand for goods and materials grew along with the demand for Icelandic and Greenlandic goods in Europe. Valborg was becoming a very rich man.

Unndis had gotten past the honeymoon stage

in her marriage when she began to learn that Brian was not the kind of husband her father was. When they set up their own home in a Reykjavik neighborhood, she found Brian to be rather demanding of her while sloughing off many of his own responsibilities.

He never picked up after himself but demanded she keep their small home clean with food on the table the minute he walked in. He forbade her taking time away from their home to visit her family, yet he insisted they frequently visit his family in another part of the growing town. Whenever she confronted him about his demands, he threatened to hit her.

"Husband, you have refused my requests to go visit my family three times while insisting we spend two days a week at your father's house. Tomorrow I am taking a horse and starting for my family's farm. I will be gone ten days. There is stew prepared that will feed you any days you do not wish to go to your father's house." Unndis said it in a way that was final.

"You will not do that, you ungrateful whore. You just want to get away from under me so you can go rut under some sheep farmer!" He glared at her, daring her to contradict him.

"You know that is not true. I married you for life, and you know it."

"I don't know any such thing. Ever since I provided this hall for you, you've been trying get me to let you leave. No, you will not go anyplace unless I allow it. Furthermore, you will come over here, get down on your knees, apologize for insulting me by your silly requests, and beg for forgiveness."

"I cannot believe I am hearing this! I wait on you hand and foot, and all you do is make more demands."

Without hesitation, he reached out and cuffed the side of her head. She fell onto her side, saw stars, and was disoriented.

"You will not lay another hand on me!" she screamed.

His blood was up, and he started for her. Her reaction was to send a fast-moving foot into his groin. He doubled over and started to throw up. He looked at her with hate in his eyes. "You are a dead woman," he coughed.

She rolled back, got to her feet and drove a knee into his broad face. Blood gushed from his nose. He wiped his nose on his sleeve, stood and came after her. She dodged, slipped under the table and came up by the hearth, grabbing a pan in one hand and a butcher knife in the other.

He cackled a menacing laugh, drew a belt knife, and threw it at her. She deflected it with the pan, but the blade pierced her sleeve and stuck in her upper arm.

Seeing her hurt, he charged. A big fist was drawn back to hit her in the face. With a weakening arm, she drew the pan up to stop his punch. His clenched fist hit the pan with a clang and crack as bones in his hand broke. The pan flew back and hit her in the shoulder, twisting her body around.

As she flailed for balance, her butcher knife sliced deep into the forearm attached to his broken hand. Blood gushed from the wound.

"You've kilt me!" he screamed.

"You promise not to attack me again, and I will see if I can stop the bleeding." There was no compassion in her voice.

"'Tis dizzy what I be feelin'." The seriousness of his wound started to set in.

With his knife still stuck in her arm, she wrapped a rag around his arm just above his elbow, tied a large cooking spoon to it and began twisting it in a circle. Soon the blood flow slowed, and finally stopped. He had passed out by then.

She pulled the knife from her arm, determined the damage was not serious but needed attention soon. She wrapped her wound as best she could, then cleaned up his face.

A knock on her door startled her. She stepped to the door and opened it a crack. It was Thorolf Magnisson, her neighbor's son. He was no older than her.

"Sorry to intrude, Unndis Brianswife, but we heard yelling and screaming followed by some crashing. My folks and I was wondering if you are all right over here." He indicated his parents looking on from in front of their hall.

"It's my husband. He attacked me, but I was able to hurt him worse, I believe." Unndis was not sure who got the worse end of their fight. She never dreamed that an argument with her husband would get so carried away so quickly. *How did I not see this side of him in the three years I have known him?*

Thorolf waved for his father to come, then turned to Unndis. "Let me have a look at him, then I best take a good look at your arm. I think the bruise on your face will heal all right."

"Are...are you a healer of some kind?" she asked.

"No, but Father and Mother know something of healing."

About then, another knock on the door sounded.

"Step in, Father. There was a bit of a scuffle here."

"I see. Is Brian alive?" Magni asked.

"He passed out when I was tightening the tourniquet," Unndis replied.

"You probably saved his life."

Brian began to stir. Before he opened his eyes, he yelled, "You no good bitch, I will kill you for this! You deserve no sympathy from any court! A woman who cuts her husband should die of the most gruesome torture."

"Brian! It is me, Magni. You better restrain your mouth."

"She cut me, Magni. She needs to die! No woman should cut her husband. Did you know she is a Skræling whore? What did she do with my knife? I'll kill her right now!"

"Easy now, Brian. There's been enough blood spilled here today."

"I will not go easy until she dies!"

"Help me restrain him, Thorolf," Magni pleaded.

Brian was struggling to get up. In his attempt to get off the floor, Brian smacked his broken hand on the table leg. He screamed in pain as he went berserk. Thrashing, he landed a hard punch to Magni's head and knocked him unconscious.

Brian was beyond feeling pain as he shoved the helpless Magni off him and worked his way to his feet. "Where is my knife, you useless whore?" Brian started stalking through the hall.

Thorolf yelled, "Settle down, Brian, you are hurt. Let us take care of you."

"After I kill that no good Skræling whore!" He looked down and saw the handle of the butcher knife pinned under Magni's side. He bent down to wrest it out from under Magni and started to stand up. Suddenly, his world went black.

Unndis stood over Brian's body. Her wounded arm was on fire as she held the iron pan in both hands, waiting for Brian to make another move.

"I-it's all over now, Unndis. Let me get Brian off Father. If you have some cord, we'll restrain Brian, then take care of that arm of yours."

"W-what h-happened?" Magni asked when Thorolf pulled Brian's big body from him.

"He went berserk! Somehow Unndis got past me and smashed Brian's head with that pan."

"Are you all right, Unndis?" Magni asked.

"I-I d-don't k-know," she replied.

"Let's get him tied up good, in case he wakes up again. Where is that cord?" Thorolf asked Unndis.

She stepped over Brian to get to a box by the hearth. She pulled out a ball of heavy twine and handed it to Thorolf.

Well into the night, Magni, Thorolf, and Bodil Magniswife tended to Brian and Unndis's wounds. Brian needed stitches in his forearm and his hand, a wooden splint to bind his broken fingers, and a bandage on his broken nose.

Unndis needed stitches for the entry and exit wounds in her upper arm and a cold, wet cloth on her bruised face.

Magni sent Thorolf to get the local gothi to record the legal aspects. Bodil went to get the Christian priest to see about having the marriage between Brian Bagott and Unndis Torsdottir annulled due to the circumstances.

The gothi said that the gothar would be reluctant to grant an annulment if it was not recommended by the church.

Unndis asked Bodil if she could stay in their hall until this matter was brought to a conclusion.

As soon as she was able, Unndis would be moving back to Rolcarllandstedr, dowry in hand or not.

With statements from Magni and Thorolf, the local gothar court and the Christian church granted Unndis an annulment, and her dowry was returned intact. By the time she was able to make the trip back to her home, she was reluctant to leave Thorolf, who proved to be a fine young man.

———

WHEN UNNDIS RETURNED TO ROLFCARLLANDSTEDR, the men were busy cutting hay and storing it in the barn for the coming winter.

"You poor dear." Gerna hugged Unndis. "We all thought Brian was a fine man. He was hiding his anger deep."

"Yes. And when Valborg fired him, he went after his master. Luckily, one of Valborg's men was close by and restrained Brian as he was raising his knife to strike Valborg down," Unndis announced.

"We won't lack for topics to discuss at Althing next summer," said Tor.

Thorolf accompanied Unndis, and she invited him to stay a few nights. He could help with getting the hay in if he chose. He did.

The day after Thorolf returned home, the men were still in the fields cutting hay. Although his hair was turning gray, Tor insisted on working as hard as any man on the farm. That day, he, Egill, and Halvar were cutting the grasses with scythes while the other men were piling it onto the wagons with hay forks.

Erik drove his wagon up to where Tor was cutting. Three-year-old Harald sat on the seat beside him. When he stopped, Erik turned to talk to Bjorn to his left.

Tor turned to wave to his grandson. The boy stood up to look around. He lost his balance and began to tumble off the front of the wagon right behind the horse. Erik was turned to Bjorn, whose view of Harald was blocked.

Tor saw Harald begin to fall, dropped his scythe, pivoted, and ran the couple steps to the wagon. When Harald began to fall, he screamed, which frightened the horse, which reacted by stepping back.

Tor dove to his knees, grabbed Harald, and blocked the horse with his shoulder. The horse stepped sideways, and no damage was done. Erik jumped down to get Harald out of harm's way.

"Thank you, Father. I think you saved Harald's life just now."

"I just reacted. Any of us would have done the same," Tor said stoically.

Erik looked down at Tor's bloody leg. "You're hurt! How did that happen? We better get you to the house and get that looked at!"

"Nah, just a scratch," Tor proclaimed.

"I saw it," Halvar said. "When you dropped your scythe and turned after the boy, your scythe hung up in the grass and dragged across your leg. I sharpened that scythe this morning. You could shave with it."

At Erik's insistence, they loaded Tor on the wagon, on top of the soft hay, and made tracks for the hall.

When Heidi saw Tor's blood-soaked pant leg, she dropped the hoe she was weeding the garden with and ran to him.

"Everyone is making a big fuss over a little scratch!" Tor exclaimed. *It does hurt pretty bad*, he admitted to himself. Heidi saw through his façade and knew he was hurt badly.

Cairenn and Heidi cut his pant leg off below the knee right there on the wagon. They started to pull his boot off, but when they did, the cut, which was just above his boot top, opened wider. More blood flowed. Heidi did not hesitate. She used her knife to slice from the top of the boot to the sole. Then the boot slid off easily. About then, Gerna arrived with hot water, rags, bandages, a needle, and thread.

"We must clean it thoroughly," Cairenn declared.

Gerna washed while Cairenn threaded the needle and Heidi began mixing the best healing plants she knew of. She immediately gave Tor a willow twig to chew on to try to ease the pain. Cairenn had Gerna wash just in front of each stitch as she closed the deep cut. By the time Cairenn had the cut sewn tight, Heidi had a poultice ready to cover the wound and bandages to hold the poultice in place.

"Will it heal, Father?" Egor asked Egill.

"We pray it will, son. With all our hearts."

When Heidi changed the bandage and poultice that night, she was not confident. Redness along the cut was not what she wanted to see. She tried to mix the new poultice a little stronger, but she only had so much to work with. Her homeland forests harbored more healing plants than this area of Iceland.

The next morning, Tor said he was feeling a bit better. When Heidi opened the bandage, she was disheartened. The red area along the cut was wider and beginning to ooze. The leg was quite warm to the touch. She sent Gerna to get some ice from their dwindling supply in the milk room.

She packed the leg in ice, then washed and dried it again before putting on a new poultice and wrapping it. By evening, Tor was feeling feverish all over. His appetite was gone. His biggest wish was to hold Heidi's hand. She was frantically trying to find a way to break the fever.

Each time Heidi changed the bandage, the leg looked worse. The whole calf was now a mosaic of colors, none of them friendly. On the third morning after the accident, a red line followed the vein all the way from his calf to his groin before it disappeared. She knew Tor was going to die. The thought hurt more than anything in her life. He was her rock. Her refuge when all else was bad. Now she felt completely helpless. *Dear God, please don't let this good man die.* She prayed constantly. She sent Bjorn for the priest in Borg. She did not know what else to do.

The next morning, Tor's entire leg was black. His fever was unbearable. He moaned incoherently all the time. It was impossible for Heidi to cool his burning forehead. His breathing was shallow and irregular, and his jaw was locked in place. The end was near. Heidi could not rest, nor could she stay awake.

The priest arrived. He had seen this before as well. There was nothing anyone could do. "It is in God's hands. He has called brother Tor to his side. We mortals have no say in the matter."

Heidi sat by Tor's feverish body all night. Somewhere just after dawn, she awoke. She took his hand. It was cooler. She began to get hope when she looked into his lifeless eyes. Her "NO!" could be heard throughout the hall. Gerna got to her side first. Heidi was conscious, but her mind was shut down. Her graying hair was dirty and orderless. She held Tor's lifeless hand and refused to let go.

"He is at peace now, Mother. We can thank God for that. His suffering is over." Gerna hugged her mother when more words failed her.

Heidi spoke, "We always thought we would die together. Perhaps in a battle, or maybe at sea. Neither of us wanted to leave the other behind. Now, it is me who must go on. And I will." There were no tears.

Gerna sobbed uncontrollably. One by one, or two by two, the rest of the family came in to try to support Heidi. But she showed more strength than any of them.

Half of western Iceland came for the funeral at Rolfcarllandstedr. Tor had been a respected farmer and a good neighbor. Law Speaker Gellir Bolverksson spoke of the good things Tor had accomplished in his time in Iceland.

CHAPTER 22

THE DREAM

Heidi adjusted to life without Tor as best she could. She had her family around her, after all. Unndis married the good young man, Thorolf Magnisson, and they stayed on the farm. There were so many family members on the farm, she had trouble remembering all their names. *They all know what needs to be done, and someone here knows just how to do all those things. It's almost like I am the only one who is not needed here anymore. Oh well.*

"No dear. You all go on. I don't need to go to Althing this year. You have fun and bring me back something special from the fair," Heidi told Gerna.

"What's this, Heidi? You are not going to Althing? Now, we all go to Althing. Everyone is there, the whole bloomin' country. Why would ye miss it? Come, let me help ye pack your personal things," Cairenn pressed.

"I will be staying here this year, my friend. Please leave it that."

"But I be your oldest and dearest friend in the world. What will I be doin' there all by me lonesome wi'out ye? I'll be worried sick about ya is what I'll be doin' if ye stay here all alone."

"You are an old and dear friend for a fact, Cairenn. But you are not my oldest friend." Heidi glanced at the hill where Tor was buried, along with Thorkell, Hildr, and their two sons.

"But leavin' ya here all alone...would ya like me to stay with ya?"

"No, Cairenn. I wish to be alone for a spell. Maybe some good-looking young sheepherder will come along, and I'll marry him," Heidi said with finality.

All her children, and their spouses and children, said goodbye with tears in their eyes before they climbed onto a wagon or into a saddle. "You left Bright Star in the barn for me to ride, Erik?"

"Of course, Mother. No one would dare leave you here without her. I love you, Mother." Erik let a tear trickle down his face.

"Go on, all of you. The sooner you go, the sooner you'll be home, and you can tell me everything I missed. I love all of you, too!"

She stood by the hitching post and watched until the small caravan of wagons and horses left. She turned and started toward the door to the main hall. Heidi put her hand on the big door latch...and stopped. She turned and walked up the hill to Tor's grave.

"Maybe we can have that talk now. That one where you wanted me to tell you about my dreams. They are wonderful dreams, my husband. I go back to my sister's village. We talk. Mostly about family. Some things there I think you would be interested to know. I have a niece who is a great warrior. She has killed many enemies. Those northern Haudenosaunee people keep trying to push our people out. My niece calls herself Cass. Imagine that! She has made many warriors wish they had not come to our lands.

"And I have a nephew who built a bark canoe, filled it with trade goods, and has left to be a wandering trader. Traveler is his hero.

"Wouldn't you love to see those people again? I kept from telling you because I was afraid to would get some silly notion that we could go back there. It never was possible to go back, my husband. We became different people. Our path was ordained by God. He wanted someone to come here to tell of the good things over there. But not even God could make most of these people see.

"I am not sad we could not make the trade work. My people would have been polluted by the bad people here. They would want the metal weapons and do whatever was needed to get them. They would have murdered friends and torn asunder alliances. They would learn to see the wolf and the bear as an enemy instead of a brother. With metal axes, they would cut the tress down, just like the Norse did here. It is the way of people. Greed destroys everything our earth mother has built.

"So, I am happy that we came here. My eyes have seen what will happen. Yes, because someday, all these people will find what wonderful things are there, and they will overwhelm the true people and all be lost.

"But we have seen both and can live with ourselves, knowing we did not open the gate to the destruction of my people. Thank you, my husband, for learning that our task was to learn and try to educate. But by failing, we kept a world alive, at least for now."

She closed her eyes and prayed. *Dear God, thank you for a long life filled with many wonders. Thank you for letting me witness the good and the bad in people, that I might learn to be good. I may never be worthy to go to your heaven and to walk at your side. But I have seen enough to have an idea of what that might be like. Amen.*

She looked across the pastures at the green grasses, and all the way to the snow-covered mountains to the southeast. She closed her eyes again. *Wolf, thank you for being my spirit helper. You helped me become the woman I am, or at least was. You knew I was coming here before I did. You told me you could not protect me in this land. But I think you have. Your wisdom and guidance opened my eyes to a world I could never have imagined. What I learned was that no matter where they go, men are men. Some are good and try to make their world better. But so many are greedy. Greedy for things, especially things that sparkle, greedy for power over other men, to own other men, even, greedy for sex, to dominate women, greedy to own or control land. That one is hard to understand. No one can take land with them when they cross over to the land of the ancestors, or to heaven. What is the point?*

Wolf, this will probably be the last time I pray to you. Again, thank you for all you have shown me.

Heidi sat by Tor's grave a bit longer. She talked to him some more. She told she thinks Unndis and Thorolf will have a baby soon. "I know it will be a girl. All of my children have girls. We have a legacy to pass on."

Heidi went back to the hall. She drank some crowberry juice and thought about eating but decided to wait. When darkness encroached, she took a lantern to her room, opened her bed, snuffed the light and crawled in between the blankets. She remembered sleeping naked, especially at Tor's side. *How wonderful he smelled. I think I miss that most of all. His smell. It told me all was well. I would be safe. Even when we were in danger and life was hanging by a thread.*

The next day she stepped out to greet the sun. She decided she would go to his grave and talk to Tor at sunrise every day while the children were gone.

A week later, it had become an ingrained habit. She walked up the low hill and looked back down the cart track. To the east, the sun would swing along the horizon until it climbed high into the sky. It would not fully set, but her day would end sometime in the evening.

She instantly went into alert mode. Far down the track, a lone rider was coming toward her farm. She hurried to the hall and picked up her axe. She thought about her bow but knew she could no longer draw it. She went back out to the hitching post and stood like a guard, axe in hand. She could still throw it with decent speed and accuracy. I know this man on a horse is coming to this farm to harm someone, and I am the only someone here.

She watched his every step as he slowly walked the horse toward her. He was still four hundred paces away when she got an odd sense that he was familiar. As he drew closer she could see his horse was a big black. It was heavily laden. His black hair and beard looked greasy and unkempt. His black cloak was covered in dust. He was still two hundred paces out when could see that it was Brian, ex-husband of Unndis. *This is trouble.*

When he was one hundred paces out, she could see his hateful eyes. When he was fifty paces away, she could see the nose that Unndis had rearranged on his once-handsome face. Closer, he looked gaunt, like he had not been eating well.

At twenty paces, he stopped. He would have plenty of time to duck if she threw her axe at this distance.

"What do you want?" she asked in a neutral tone.

"What's mine."

"What's yours around here?"

"A wife and a dowry. For starters."

"There are no wives or dowries on this holding."

"Don't lie, woman. You're a wife. And ye have four daughters, as I recall. One of 'em is mine, and I'll be takin' her back, along wi' the dowry that be rightfully mine."

"I am not a wife. I am a widow. And my four daughters have gone to Althing, along with their four husbands. Your marriage to my Unndis was annulled by the church and the state, and the dowry was returned to Unndis, the rightful owner. So, it seems you have come a long way for nothing. If you hurry you can get back to Borg before twilight sets in."

"I'll be goin' nowhere until I get what's mine. Why don't you hurry on into your big hall and make me a meal. Maybe I will let you share my bed tonight. You still look pretty spry for a grandmother."

"Brian, you are making a mistake. Now, just turn around and be gone."

"You really are a stupid Skræling whore, aren't you? You are the one making a mistake. You're a frail old woman. I will overpower you and hurt you badly. Then what? You going to wait on the floor with a mess of broken bones for your four daughters and their four husbands to come along and rescue you?" He eased his horse a little closer as he talked.

She subtly stepped so she was partially behind the big hitching post. He started to step down from the saddle.

"Just stay in that saddle, Brian. You don't want to dig your hole any deeper than it is. Just ride out of here and be gone, forever."

"I have a better idea." He stepped quickly off the horse, turned, and started quickly toward her, hand reaching out like he was going for her axe.

She sidestepped, drew the axe back, and slammed it into the side of his neck. He looked at her in disbelief as the strength quickly left his legs. Blood gushed in a fountain of pulsing blood from the side of his neck. He dropped to the ground, twitched a few times, and was still.

Great, now I have a body to dispose of. It will be badly decomposing by the time the children return. It was more than a league to a place where there were some eroded gullies where she could bury him deep enough that the foxes could not dig him up.

I will drag him half a league out to the north. First I will strip him and his horse of all their gear and tack. I will tie him to his horse and have the animal drag his carcass to the open plain and strip his clothes off. Then, I will talk nicely to the horse and slide a stiletto into its neck. The foxes will make quick work of all that meat. There will be little left but bones when I explain things to Gothi Bjorn.

After she had disposed of Brian Bagott's body, Heidi settled into a routine of existing. The high-light of each day was her sunrise talk with Tor. He agreed that she had no choice but to kill Brian. And she had no logical way to bury his body. A few days after she left the carcasses to the foxes, she rode Bright Star out to see what had taken place. There was a flock of about fifty ravens fighting with foxes over the scraps that were left. The horse's skeleton was fairly intact, but the man's was widely scattered.

At last, the day came when she expected her

family to return. She went through her routine of telling Tor she was kind of excited that the children might be back that day or the next. Little did she know they had left a day and a half early and would get to the farm about midday.

She went to sit in her usual spot next to Tor and began telling him about all she would tell the children. She needed their son-in-law to make a report explaining what happened with Brian. As she was telling Tor about that, the sun seemed to be pulsing through thin clouds to the east. The strange, pulsing light took her attention, and she just looked on.

Behind the pulsing light, a shape began to appear. It was the mountain in her dreams. But now it was winter. Snow was falling and being drive by high winds up and over the peak. As she lowered her gaze, pines dominated the higher elevations, then trees that shed their leaves. Snow was piled high on the ground under the gray trees. Further down the slope, a few hemlocks poked from the gray mass of leafless trees.

With the blowing snow and gray sky, it was hard to see smoke rising from the village. When the palisade came into view, the contrasting blue/gray smoke became easier to see. With the wind howling and snow blowing, she was not surprised to see no sentries or other activities happening outside the longhouses.

She went straight to the Water Plant Clan long-house and slipped inside the double-thick elk hide door hanging. The place was packed. She recognized all her old friends. This time, only Corn Stalk, Traveler, and a few other elders had gray streaks in their hair. Everyone looked to be about the age they were when she and Tor were last here.

Her sister had black hair. She had a toddler boy on her hip and another baby by her in a cradleboard. Red Hand was talking to Tallow, and Water Mint was talking to Corn Stalk. Traveler saw her and walked over and stood in front of her.

"Where is Yellow Hair?" Traveler asked.

"He was not able to come," she answered.

"Too bad. I wanted to ask him how my canoe is holding up."

"We had to sell it. It was part of the trade to get us to the land of the Micmac and to the bay where the Norse Canoe was," she said.

"I see," he said thoughtfully. "I will not take any more of your time."

"Wait. I heard that my nephew wants to be a trader, like you."

"Not for a few more years. As you can see, he is a bit too young at this time."

"Right." She looked at her sister with the toddler climbing on her. She turned back and Traveler was nowhere to be seen.

Next, Water Mint came to her. "Did you find Yellow Hair's People?"

"Yes!"

"What are they like?"

"Like people everywhere. There are good ones and bad ones. Most just want to work and get along. The greedy ones spoil it for everyone."

"Is that what you have learned?"

"Yes."

"You could have learned that here without going there."

"Could I?" Heidi saw Water Mint look away. She followed her aunt's gaze. Tallow and Red Hand were talking.

When Heidi turned back to Water Mint, she was nowhere to be seen. She stepped over to Bright Star.

"Sister, you are back. I knew you would come back! But where is Yellow Hair? He did not abandon you in some far away land, did he?"

"No. He just could not be here."

"What about children?"

"They could not come, either."

"But you could. That makes my heart sing."

"Are you head matron yet?"

"No! Water Mint likes being head matron more than she ever thought she would. But that is all right. I am too young to be a head matron yet. These two are a handful. And if Red Hand has his way, there will be more!"

"My heart sings for you!"

"So, what children do you have?"

"My children are grown. Two have children of their own, the other three are pregnant."

"Five grown children. How old are you?"

"Same age as you, forty-five."

"And Yellow Hair?"

"Well, he died. He had an accident and evil spirits invaded his body."

"If your children are grown and your husband has died, there is no need for you to go back. You can stay here. It will be just like it used to be."

"I suppose you are right."

When Gerna saw the dried blood on the hitch post. She became worried for Heidi. Then, she looked to the hill where her father was buried. She saw a dark lump by the grave of Tor. She ran to the clump to discover her mother. She was alive and had an enigmatic smile on her face. Gerna called for Bjorn and Erik to carry Mother to her bed. They got to her bed and found it neatly made with her nightdress folded and laying on top.

Gerna, Erna, Gerdis, and Unndis got their mother out of her dress, into her night dress, and into bed. Heidi was limp the whole time. They snuffed the lantern and left her alone.

It was quite late when everything was put away. Everyone was ready for bed. Gerna checked on Heidi and found no change.

Erik came in and said there was strange gear, a saddle, and tack in the barn. Among the items was a balanced throwing knife. Unndis looked at that knife, and her eyes bugged out in surprise.

"That knife was Brian's," Unndis whispered.

AUTHOR'S NOTE

The story of Tor Eriksson, a.k.a. Yellow Hair, and Bright Moon, a.k.a. Cass, a.k.a. Heidr Tungl, a.k.a. Heidi Torswife, comes to an end. But their legacy lives on among the residents of Iceland. Modern DNA evidence indicates a woman of North American origin made her way to Iceland in the first half of the eleventh century and gave birth to at least four daughters who have passed a mitochondrial DNA marker down to a small population of modern Icelanders. This story has presented a hypothetical story of how that may have taken place.

Along the way, a few historical figures have been mentioned. For instance, the Icelandic Law Speakers mentioned in the text were the real persons according to historical records. However, all accounts of their activities in this story are the product of the author's imagination.

Also, please note that, although Yellow Hair and Bright Moon have passed on, they left close friends and family behind along the Spirit Water (Allegheny) River. The Yellow Hair series continues with the stories of Heidi's nephew and niece in their struggles to survive in a land that was experiencing social and political change long before the arrival of European colonists.

Follow the story of Red Bone, who emulates the life of his hero, Traveler, the great trader. Red Bone's travels spanned the world of Turtle Island, drawing him into conflicts and political upheaval from coast to coast.

Finally, follow the story of how a new Bright Moon reclaims her aunt's name and legacy as a great warrior defending her family, village, and the Monongahela Nation as external pressures threaten to end their precarious hold on their beloved homeland.

A LOOK AT BOOK SEVEN
REDBONE

A boy born with a broken step dares to dream beyond the confines of his village.

In a world where warriors define honor through battle, Redbone's club foot sets him apart. Inspired by tales from Traveler, an aging trader, Redbone discovers his strength in trade, not combat. Armed with a canoe and unwavering determination, he sets out to explore the rivers of Turtle Island.

His journey takes an unexpected turn when he meets Red Petal, a quick-witted Lenni Lenape woman fleeing a scandal. Together, they brave treacherous waters, journey to the bustling city of Cahokia, and face the challenges of the Shining Mountains. But danger looms as enemies close in, including a ruthless Cheyenne chief whose wrath could shatter their bond.

Will Redbone's spirit guide him to a life of purpose, or will the untamed rivers claim him?

Set in eleventh-century North America, Redbone *is perfect for fans of historical fiction steeped in danger and discovery.*

AVAILABLE MARCH 2025

ABOUT THE AUTHOR

Ron Briggs is a veteran, having served four years in the USAF. His education includes a Bachelor of Science in Range and Wildlife Ecology at Oklahoma State University and a Master of Science in Range and Wildlife Management at Texas A&I University.

He is retired from the USDA-Natural Resources Conservation Service, and his career encompassed twenty-five years as District Conservationist in Linn County, Kansas. Prior to college, he worked seven years in the building trades.

Having developed a deep interest in history, especially in the pre-colonial period of North America, Ron's interests prompted him to begin researching a pre-history story about the Tallgrass Prairie Region of the Great Plains. That research evolved into his current multi-volume work, the Yellow Hair series, which includes scenes from northern Europe to the mountains of western North America.

Ron and his wife, Debbie, currently live in Mound City, Kansas, and have two grown children and seven grandchildren. His interests include spending time with family, writing, hunting, fishing, traveling, and woodworking.

BIBLIOGRAPHY

Appelt, Martin. "Man, Culture and Environment in Ancient Greenland," *Publication No. 4*, Danish Polar Center.

Bierhorst, John. *Mythology of the Lanape: Guide and Texts.* University of Arizona Press, 1995.

Bronsted, Johannes. *The Vikings.* Penguin Books, London, 1960, revised 1965.

Byock, Jesse. "The Icelandic Althing: Dawn of Parliamentary Democracy," *Heritage and Identity: Shaping the Nations of the North*, ed. J.M. Fladmark, pp. 1–18. The Hayerdahl Institute and Robert Gordan University. Donhead St. Mary, Shaftsbury, 2002

Clarke, Helen and Bjorn Ambrosiani. *Towns in the Viking Age.* St. Martin's Press, New York, 1991.

Cohat, Yves and Ruth Daniel, tr. *The Vikings: Lords of the Seas.* Gallimard, 1987.

Damas, David. *Arctic, Vol. 5, Handbook of North American Indians.* Smithsonian Press, Washington, D.C., 1984.

Charles River Editors. *Native American Tribes: The History and Culture of the Inuit (Eskimos).*

Feasel, Charles T. *White Bear.* Ballantine Books, New York, 1990.

Fitzhugh, William and Elizabeth Ward. *Vikings, The North Atlantic Saga.* Smithsonian Press, Washington, D.C., 2000.

Gordon, E. V., rev. by A. R. Taylor, A. R. *An Introduction to Old Norse.* Oxford Press, London.

Gronnow, Bjarni. *Late Dorset in High Arctic Greenland: Final Report on the Gateway to Greenland Project.* Canadian Archeological Association, 1999.

Grumet, Robert S. *The Lenapes (Indians of North America).* Chelsea House Publishing, 1989.

Harrington, Mark R. *Religion and Ceremonies of the Lenape.* Forgotten Books, 2012.

Harrington, Mark R. *The Indians of New Jersey, Dickon Among the Lanapes.* Rutgers University Press, New Jersey, 1966.

Heckewelder, John and Ernestus Gotlieb, notes by William C. Reichel. *History, Manners, and Customs of The Indian Nations Who Inhabited Pennsylvania and the Neighbouring States.* Historical Society of Pennsylvania, 1881.

Ingstad, Anne Stine et al. *The Discovery of a Norse Settlement in America. Excavations at L'Anse aux Meadows, Newfoundland, 1961-1968.* Tromso, 1977.

Jakobsson, Sverrir. "The Process of State Formation in Medieval Iceland." www.academia.edu, 2001.

Jones, Gwynne. *A History of the Vikings.* Oxford University Press, 1968, 1973, 1984.

Kunz, Keneva, tr., Gisli Sigurdsson, ed. *The Vinland Sags.* Penguin Books, London, 2008.

McCullough, K. M. "The Ruin Islanders: Thule Culture Pioneers in the High Eastern Arctic." Archeological Survey of Canada, 141, Canadian Museum of Civilization, 1989.

McGee, Robert. *Ancient People of the Arctic.* University of British Columbia Press, Vancouver, 1996.

McGee, Robert. *The Last Imaginary Place.* Oxford University Press, New York, 2005.

Mcleod, William Christi. "The Family Hunting Territory and Lenape Political Organization," American Anthropology 24.

Maschner, Herbert, Owen Masson, and Robert McGee. *The Northern World AD 900-1400.* The University of Utah Press, Salt Lake City, 2009.

Maxwell, Moreau S. Prehistory of the Eastern Arctic. Academic Press, New York, 1985.

Means, Bernard K. *Circular Villages of the Monongahela Tradition.* The University of Alabama Press, Tuskaloosa, 2007.

Rasmusen, Knud. *Eskimo Folk Tales*. Gyldendal, Copenhagen, 1921.

Roesdahl, Else. *The Vikings*. Penguin Books, New York, 1987.

Schledermann, Peter. *Crossroads to Greenland, 3000 Years of Prehistory in the Eastern High Arctic*. The Arctic Institute of North America of the University of Calgary, 1990.

Seaver, Kirsten A. *The Frozen Echo, Greenland and the Exploration of North America, ca. A.D. 1000-1500*. Stanford University Press, Stanford, CA, 1996.

Simpson, Jacqueline. *Everyday Life in the Viking Age*. Dorset Press, New York, 1967.

Sutherland, Patricia, ed. *Contributions to the Study of Dorset Paleo Eskimos*. Canada Museum of History, 2005.

Trigger, Bruce G. *Northeast, Vol 15, Handbook of North American Indians*. Smithsonian Institution Press, Washington, D.C., 1984.

Weslager, C. A. *The Delaware Indians: A History*. Rutgers University Press, New Jersey, 1972.

www.ingramcontent.com/pod-product-compliance
Lightning Source LLC
Chambersburg PA
CBHW012035140726
47990CB00010B/3242